HERO AD LITEM

HERO AD LITEM

888-555-HERO #10

SUZAN HARDEN

This is a work of fiction. All characters, organizations and events in this story are products of the author's imagination and are not to be construed as real. Any resemblance to persons, living or dead, is entirely coincidental.

Published by Angry Sheep Publishing
Findlay, Ohio

Interior Design by JW Manus
Cover Design by For the Muse Design

*For the late George Perez, who taught me a lot
about storytelling and found families*

CHAPTER 1

A month ago

Byron S. Trubble would have laughed if his life didn't depend on his silence. The old battleax and her stooges thought they'd broken him. He'd only given one real name of one kid from sixty years ago and his alleged location to Peggy Reinhold. One of the kids that died in a training accident. The rest of the information he supposedly spilled was total bullshit.

If anyone should have known that torture wasn't a reliable method of extracting information, it should have been the woman who used to be Rue Liberty.

And if she were smarter, she would have recruited more people with powers than just her daughter. Maybe even a telepath to dig through his head.

Like he had when he ran Corvus.

He slunk along the dry limestone wall. The fishy smell meant he was getting close to the bunker's entrance.

His last escape attempt failed because he was stupid enough to believe the new Ghost Owl was Pablo Inunza's son. Nope, with the power set, it had to be the Garcia kid's twin brother. With their ties to the Winters and Franklin law firm, the goodie-two-shoes brothers should have had Professor Venom trace his call to Aisha Franklin.

What if the bitch didn't tell them about his call? What if he really miscalculated and Franklin was part of Reinhold's little organization?

Trubble exhaled heavily. If he wanted to keep breathing, he needed to move. He stepped into the night and waited for his vision to adjust. Beneath the moonlight, rust coated the steel escape stairs. The damn things were nearly as old as he was. One step onto them, and he could plummet into the Rio Cristo fifty feet below. Assuming he didn't hit a rock on the way down, the rapids would drown him.

However, free-hand rock climbing a canyon wall in the dark was an even stupider option.

Trubble grabbed the railing.

He didn't touch rust. It felt more like paint. He gently flicked the railing with his forefinger and snickered at the bell tone. The old biddy had replaced the escape stairs and painted them to look like they were the original decrepit ones.

Still, he tapped the landing with his foot in the stolen boot to make sure. Yep, damn solid.

Trubble eased down the steps, not out of worry of plummeting to his death, but so the sentries above and the possible ones below didn't hear him. He could handle a couple of punks as long as they weren't supers.

Air came in short, desperate gasps when he reached the trail at the bottom of the stairs. Despite his best efforts at exercise and diet, he was seventy. This getting old crap sucked, but the torture hadn't helped either. Maybe he was too stubborn to die.

Trubble chuckled at his own idiocy as he ducked under the "No Trespassing" sign. He headed north along the canyon trail for Logan Grove. Normally, the ten-mile hike would be three hours or so. With the guard drugged and in his cell, Trubble estimated he'd have four hours until they missed him.

Logan Grove might have only consisted of a few houses and a general store in the Seventies, but now, it was a decent-sized town with a vehicle or two he could steal. Then it became a matter of disappearing until he could access the money he deposited offshore.

After two hours by the moon, his legs cramped something fierce. He didn't want the break, but he couldn't afford falling out here. A thigh-high boulder provided a resting spot. He perched on it and rubbed his calves.

"Not so easy running away from your past, is it, old man?"

Trubble froze at Monica Reinhold's voice behind him. So much for his brilliant plan.

"Kill me and get it over with, Miss Purrception," he snarled. "I'm not going back with you."

Monica dropped in front of him. She had her mother's classic hourglass figure, but she was so much more . . . flexible. A matte black bodysuit with a matching cowl and boots covered her from head to toe. Eye black covered her exposed skin around her orbs.

"Tell her what she wants to know, Byron." Weariness coated her words.

"We both know the minute I do, I'm dead."

"Tell me then. I'll tell her I killed you and disposed of your body. We all get what we want."

"She's not going to believe you killed me, Monica." His breath clouded in the icy mountain air. "For your vaunted reputation as a murderer and thief, we both know you're not cold-blooded enough to kill an unarmed man."

"I've killed before," she snapped.

"An accident while defending yourself is not the same thing."

"Maybe I should toss you in the river," she said. "With that frigid mountain water, hypothermia is a fairly easy way to go."

"I can't let you do that," he said.

"What are you going to do? Kill me?" She snorted. "And everyone calls *me* a supervillain."

"What prison did we break out of?" He still wanted to

kick himself for believing Monica would team up with him. She hated his guts for taking custody of her twin daughters from her. Then Peggy stabbed him in the back to take the girls from him.

"Either you kill me or you tell me the names. Those are the only ways you get to leave here alive." Monica sounded deadly serious. There was none of her usual mockery in her tone.

"I'm not going to kill you," Trubble said, and for once, he meant it. "But I'm not betraying those people. Harriet and I made sure they were well out of your mother's reach. They lived normal lives. You and your daughters are an experiment to her."

"If you hadn't taken my girls, she wouldn't have gotten custody of them," she sneered.

"That's because Byron's a blunt instrument," a husky feminine voice said. Another dark figure landed on the trail, well out of Monica's reach. "I should have known you'd betray me, too, my dear."

"Why do you have to spoil all my games, Mother?" Monica complained. "I could have gotten the names for you if you hadn't interrupted."

"Because you're an even more sentimental idiot than he is?" Peggy Reinhold raised her arm, a gun in her hand.

"You promised I could kill him once you got the names from him," Monica screeched.

"I promise a lot of people a lot of things." Peggy's laughter was still as low and throaty as it had been fifty years ago. "Including your father. I didn't keep those vows either.

The muzzle of her gun flashed.

CHAPTER 2

Present Day

Sunday morning dawned bright and beautiful. However, Susan Kennedy was glad she wore jeans and a sweatshirt emblazoned with her law school alma mater. The light hadn't burned off all of the desert's chill fog when she exited the Lechuza Building, a little reminder that it was still technically winter.

She strolled down Sixth Street, her goal to pick up breakfast at Celia's store. Traffic was almost non-existent this early on the weekend. Two doors from the bodega, she paused in front of what would become the first of Rey, Reuben, and Emilio's restaurant empire.

"Eggsactly" had been stenciled on the largest window to the right of the door. The guys had already cut a deal with Celia for the recipes of her tamales and breakfast burritos. In addition to that revenue, Susan had found a factory to produce and package Celia's spice mix. The breakfast place would be the third new business in the Canyon Block.

The downfall of Canyon Industries after the last scion of the Canyon family was accused of murdering his wife and son twenty-two years ago had left the northeast section of the city destitute. If Rey Garcia was going to save the Canyon Block and the people who lived in it as an investor and as the superhero Black Falcon, Susan would do her damnedest to make sure he had the tools to make both happen.

She grinned as she peered through the glass. Her next door neighbor Miguel Esperanza and his construction crew had done a fine job on the interior. Miguel respected the Art Deco designs of the surviving Canyon Block buildings. He worked with the architecture instead of making the storefront something it wasn't meant to be.

"Susan?"

She slowly pivoted. The tall, dark-haired man behind her wore khakis and a polo beneath a navy windbreaker. Dark glasses shielded his eyes from the rising sun. None of which disguised the fact he was her law partner Harri Winters' ex-husband, FBI Special Agent Edward Lewis.

"Doesn't Sarah have an electric shock collar on you that goes off if you come to the Canyon Block, Eddie?"

A whisper of a smile floated across his face. "I'm still one hundred yards away from Harri. Besides, I heard through the grapevine she and Tim tied the knot over New Year's weekend."

"Is your current wife okay now that your ex-wife is hitched?"

Eddie chuckled. "Not one bit." He sobered. "Unfortunately, I'm here on business. My boss wants your opinion on something."

Susan folded her arms. "And why isn't Special Agent in Charge Consuelo contacting Harri?"

"Because she needs someone who can keep their cool, and we both know Harri's not the most level-headed attorney at Winters and Franklin."

"And because Aisha's in Paris."

Eddie shrugged.

Crap. Susan expected something to hit the fan once the Garcia-Franklins left for Europe, but a summons by the head of the Canyon Pointe FBI on a Sunday morning was not going to be good. She eyed Eddie. "Can I get some breakfast first?"

"Depends. How strong is your stomach?"

Nope, definitely not good.

"Shouldn't you be calling in the NSB and a super?"

He gestured further down the street. She looked to her left.

Past the traffic light, another federal agent stood by a parked blue SUV. The woman was dressed similarly to Eddie, but she wore the black windbreaker of the National Superhero Bureau. The firm's client Qiang Reilly AKA Sparx stood next to the agent. However, Qiang wore civilian clothing. Both woman were watching Susan with frowns on their faces.

Crap. This was really, *really* bad if the FBI and the NSB were working together on this one.

"Let me grab a tea at Celia's for the ride if you want a coherent legal opinion."

———•———

Three hours later, Susan watered some sage brush with her tea. When she was sure she had nothing left in her stomach, she wiped her mouth on the back of her sweatshirt sleeve.

"Want some water to wash out the taste?" Qiang held out a bottle for her.

"Thanks." Susan unscrewed the cap, took a swig, and swished the liquid around her mouth before she spit out the water in the direction of her vomit.

"First body?" the superhero asked sympathetically.

"How'd you guess?" Susan said bitterly.

The NSB's special agent in charge for Canyon Pointe Wilbur Nesmith approached them. Susan had never seen the sixty-something man in less than a full suit, and he didn't disappoint, even though they were in the middle of the Polvo de Oro Desert.

"You okay, Ms. Kennedy?"

"Just peachy." She took a small sip of water to ease the ache in her stomach. "I am questioning your intelligence. You don't need me or Ms. Reilly out here. You need a good forensics team and a lab." She waved toward the techs who were taking samples of everything on and around the corpse. "For all you know, this was a hiker or a motorist who got lost."

The FBI's special agent in charge Sylvia Consuelo joined them. "I would have preferred the Ghost Owl, but they're out of pocket at the moment. You two are the next best thing we've got."

"This is the one Sunday a month I have to run personal errands," Qiang growled. "I'm the last person to suggest Harri be involved, but there's obviously a reason you don't want her here. I suggest you spill before I start electrocuting people."

There was only one person about whom either government official would be reluctant to contact Harri.

"Oh, my god," Susan whispered. "You think that's Byron Trubble, don't you?"

The look Nesmith and Consuelo exchanged said she was right.

"So he was stupid and died out here." Qiang threw up her hands. "You found him. You saved the taxpayers a buttload of money by not having to send him back to prison. Case closed. It's Miller time."

"Not exactly." Nesmith scratched his chin.

"It looks like two bullet wounds to the back of the head," Consuelo said.

"How do you know for sure?" Susan demanded. "With that much decomposition—"

"I used to work in the Las Vegas office." The FBI agent smirked. "I've seen more than my share of shallow graves in a desert."

Susan glanced at the techs before she returned her attention back to the federal agents. "I still don't understand what you want from us."

"Has Harri ever mentioned her grandmother's involvement with Eagle Forever?" Nesmith asked.

"No," Qiang blurted.

"Mrs. Winters donated to his charities, but you have access to her tax returns." Susan scowled at Nesmith and Consuelo. "Where are you going with this?"

"Considering Carol Inunza is doing time for attempted murder, that leaves two suspects who would want Trubble dead," Consuelo said.

"Then I suggest you start with the supervillain who abducted him," Susan shot back.

Qiang lowered her voice even though no one was near them. "You don't think Trubble authorized the hit on Eagle Forever, and Seismic Shift was acting on someone else's orders."

Again, the two agents exchanged looks that admitted everything.

"So why not ask Harri about her grandmother directly?" Susan asked.

"One, we don't want her going on one of her half-cocked crusades," Consuelo grumbled. "Do you have any idea how many reports have crossed my desk that mention her name?"

"Two, we wanted to give someone at the Lechuza Building forewarning." Nesmith's gray hair fluttered in the chill breeze coming down off the mountains. "Lyle Baxter-Murray, aka Judge Pablo Inunza, wasn't the only suspected super child who disappeared fifty years ago. We know Trubble was hunting them. And we also know an unknown party was hunting those kids, too. We think Eagle Forever was helping those families hide their kids, including his own daughter and grandson."

"What does this have to do with Mrs. Winters?" Susan asked.

Nesmith blew out a gusty breath. "We're concerned our third party may go after your law partner on the mistaken belief she knows something. We have reason to believe her grandmother was funding Eagle Forever's Underground Railroad for supers."

CHAPTER 3

<hr>

Monday morning, Harri Winters' eyelids popped open, and she rolled over on her back. Some wrongness had infiltrated her sleep. No, it was the absence of something.

It was still dark outside. She was in her own bed in her own bedroom in her loft from the greenish glow of her alarm clock. Her husband Tim lay beside her, snoring slightly. She inhaled deeply.

That was it. A lack of coffee aroma from the loft across the hall. Even though Rey didn't drink the beverage himself, he always got up early to make Aisha a pot of coffee.

Tim jerked upright. "What's wrong?"

Harri chuckled. "I never realized how much we depended on Rey to start our own days."

Tim groaned and flopped down on the mattress. "This is why we should get a coffee pot with a timer."

She cuddled against his side and pulled the covers over them both. "Can't you install a timer on our current coffee maker?"

"I could." He wrapped his arms around her and squeezed. "But it's kind of a waste of my talents considering coffee pots with timers are already on the market." He yawned.

"It's too quiet with them gone," she murmured. "I kind of wished Molly would have taken the Garcias' offer to loft-sit while they're in France just for the noise."

Tim laughed. "You want her throwing parties across the hall?"

"That's not what I meant."

"When does Aisha start back to work?"

"Today," Harri said. "I don't think it's her being gone that bothers me as much as missing some of our godson's milestones. Mitch will be walking by the time they return to the states."

"Let's just pray he's not flying yet when they get back," Tim said. "Regular parents do not realize how fast toddlers can be. If Mitch ends up with Rey and Aisha's power set, he'll be hell to deal with."

"Locks on the cookie jar?"

"I was thinking more of a titanium-reinforced safe for all the junk food."

Harri giggled at the idea. "You could probably sell that to a ton of parents."

"Heck, I could use one to keep you from eating all my Girl Scout cookies next month."

"I said I was sorry!"

"Prove it."

She rolled on top of him and launched her very thorough apology.

—•—

Later that morning, Harri took her first sip from her second cup of coffee when the intercom buzzed. She glanced at the two clocks displayed on the corner of her laptop's monitor. Nine a.m. in Canyon Pointe equated to five p.m. in Paris. Aisha was right on time.

Harri jabbed the intercom button. "Yes?"

"Cathy Blanchett from Family Court Number Four is on line one for you," Patty Ames chirped. Their paralegal, receptionist and all around Girl Friday was the only person at the firm who was more of a morning person than Harri.

"Thanks. If Aisha calls while I'm on the phone with the court, tell her I'll call her back in a few minutes."

"Sure thing," Patty said.

Harri picked up the receiver and punched the flashing button. "Hey, Cathy, what can I do for you?"

"It's your turn to play ad litem," the court clerk replied.

"Already?" Harri sat back in her chair. "I just signed up in December." In fact, her husband, her foster siblings, and all her staff insisted she volunteer as an ad litem in the family courts. Apparently, everyone was fed up with her mothering them.

"The judge needs someone with supers experience, Harri." Cathy sighed. "The parents are in the middle of an ugly divorce, and she wants someone who will actually look out for the kid."

"Are the parents supers?" Harri straightened in her chair and flipped her legal pad to a clean page.

"Nope, but they're both looking at the kid as a meal ticket, which is why there's a huge battle for custody." Cathy paused a second before she added, "Harri, if you don't take custody of him, you know the NSB will. Special Agent Nesmith said they'd back off if you are assigned as ad litem. He was adamant no one else would do."

Special Agent Wilbur Nesmith had become a particular thorn in Harri's backside. He was doing his damnedest to earn the firm's trust. But someone within the National Superhero Bureau had set up Rey to be abducted and experimented on by Professor Paranoia, so trust of the NSB didn't come easy to anyone at Winters and Franklin.

And Harri knew she'd be lying to herself if she thought Rey, Aisha, and Mitch were totally safe from the U.S. government while they were in France.

"All right." She sighed. "I'm assuming you already made arrangements for me to meet with the kid?"

"The next hearing is scheduled for two this afternoon to decide who gets temporary custody," Cathy said. "Can you be here?"

"Nothing like waiting until the last minute," Harri grumbled. "Yes, I'll be there. How old is he?"

"Thirteen."

Line 2 started blinking on Harri's phone set.

"Cathy, can you shoot me a copy of the file by e-mail? I've got an international call scheduled for now."

"Sure thing," the court clerk chirped. "See you at two."

Harri clenched her teeth. If this kid's case didn't keep her mind off her godson, nothing else on earth would.

CHAPTER 4

Aisha tapped her free fingers on the antique secretary desk in the tiny room serving as her office in the flat she and Rey had rented in Paris. Calling it a room was generous. She had a suspicion the previous tenants used it as a closet.

But for a closet, she couldn't fault the view. The Eiffel Tower rose over the City of Lights less than three miles away. It made for a lovely evening walk with her husband and son. This was so much better than accompanying her dad on his digs in Mexico and Central America.

She smiled to herself. Definitely far less mosquitoes.

"How's the jet-setting?" Harri chirruped over the phone receiver. Marriage was obviously agreeing with her, but Aisha didn't dare say that thought out loud.

She laughed. "I wish I was actually jet-setting. This apartment may have been furnished, but there was still a lot of stuff we needed. I think we're finally situated."

"Hey, girl!" Susan called out. "Eat a few real croissants for me!"

"I will." Aisha glanced at her notes before she launched into the status of her ongoing cases.

When she finished, Harri blurted, "How'd you get all that work done?"

"We found an au pair. And before you start bitching, she's a super herself. I've already vetted her, and she's awesome, so don't ruin this for me."

"All right," Harri drawled, "What's the catch?"

"Her parents are Lightstreak and Raindrop. The parents want me to meet with their attorneys in London about doing some licensing in the U.S. for them. They were highly impressed with my Captain Justice and Sparx campaigns." Aisha couldn't keep the sour note out of her voice. Nearly two years after Captain Justice's "death", her husband's first alter ego was still haunting her career.

"What firm in the U.K.?" Harri demanded.

"And what kind of split are we talking about?" Susan asked.

"Amblehurst, Mintegue, and Trott in London, and the split is part of what we need to negotiate. The partners want a face-to-face meeting with me tomorrow depending on how you two feel about this."

"It doesn't hurt to talk to them," Susan said.

Harri remained ominously silent.

"Harri, talk to me."

"What if they are trying to poach you?"

Crap, her best friend's insecurities were back. "Harri, I

am not leaving Winters and Franklin. We all have worked too hard. And you know damn well Rey's not going to throw away his plan to revitalize the Canyon Block. Either we cut ourselves a decent deal or we walk. It doesn't hurt anything to hear their proposal."

"It sounds like we may need another associate before you get back," Susan said.

Harri snorted. "That's assuming this thing in London goes through."

"Girl, you already promised us a second associate before I get back to Canyon Pointe," Aisha said gently. "Travis, Patty, and the intern squad don't count. Besides, expanding the firm into the international market is not a bad thing."

"I don't want us to get overwhelmed again before I can find more help," Harri said. "Plus, I was assigned my first ad litem case in the family courts this morning."

"That's great!" Aisha exclaimed at the same time as Susan.

"We'll see. He's a kid with powers, and I'll meet him for the first time this afternoon."

"Let's take everything one step at a time." Aisha picked up her pencil. "Now, about the split between firms . . ."

⎯ ⋆ ⎯

It was another hour before Aisha could finally hang up the phone. Despite Harri's fear of abandonment rearing its ugly head, she'd actually come up with some excellent points that needed to be broached with the partners at Amblehurst, Mintegue, and Trott.

She exited her tiny office to find Mitch in his high chair in the kitchenette, munching on cut banana pieces while Rey cooked.

"Mamamama!" her son shrieked when saw her. Mitch waved his arms, forgetting he had fruit chunks in his hands. The banana nuggets sailed into the air.

With the application of a little superspeed, Aisha caught the flying fruit before they landed on the floor and placed them back on the high chair tray. She bent and kissed his forehead. "Sometimes, I think you do that on purpose, baby-cakes."

Mitch grabbed one of the saved banana pieces and shoved it into his mouth.

She walked over and pecked her husband on his lips. "How was you first day of school?"

"Not too bad." He grinned as he reached around her to grab a cup of shredded carrots and dumped them into the sauté pan with the cut up chicken. "How're Harri and Susan surviving without you?"

"Harri got her first ad litem case in the family court to-day."

"Good. She needs something to focus on besides missing you." Rey kissed Aisha again while he reached for something else behind her.

She laughed. "You know you could simply tell me I'm in your way."

"But if you move, I can't kiss you every time I need something." He poured a dollop of soy sauce in the pan and stirred. "So Harri didn't freak out about the meeting in London tomorrow?"

"A little. But it was a perfectly valid worry about us overextending the firm again." Aisha walked over to sit next to Mitch at their little table.

"You mean she managed to produce a genuine reason in the middle of her anxiety attack," Rey said.

"True," Aisha replied. Mitch took advantage of her open mouth and thrust a banana chunk between her teeth. After she chewed and swallowed, she smiled at him. "Thank you, kind sir."

"And you're comfortable with Delphine being here alone with Mitch all day tomorrow?"

She made a face at her husband. "Are you trying to make me paranoid?"

"I'm just thinking maybe we should have asked Molly to come with us." Rey pulled the kitchen towel from his shoulder and wiped his hands. "She's been Mitch's nanny since you ended your maternity leave. And Patty needs Dajon to take care of Grace, especially if she's going back to school this fall."

"I'm very aware of all that," Aisha said dryly. "But you

and Patty are moving on with your educations. It's time Molly does the same. And I do trust Delphine."

"Good." Rey turned and gave the chicken and carrots another stir before he added the cup of peas. He faced Aisha again. "I don't think I could handle both you and Harri freaking out over our au pair at the same time, even if one of you is half a world away."

"I didn't freak out," she protested.

"Then if you're not freaking out, why don't you take the train to London tonight after dinner?"

"Really?"

"Baby, we both know you're not a morning person." Rey grinned. "Staying in a hotel tonight will give you some sleep-in time tomorrow. And if you get done early, you can do a little sight-seeing before the return trip back to Paris."

"But Mitch—"

"I think I can handle our son by myself for one night." Rey walked over to the table. "Besides, I think you could use the break. We both know you've been doing legal stuff despite allegedly taking two weeks off to get us settled in the city."

She grinned up at him. "You are the best husband ever."

"I know," he said before he leaned over and kissed her while Mitch clapped his hands.

CHAPTER 5

<hr>

"Sounds like she's on top of things," Susan said after Harri punched the button to end the call.

"Yep." Harri nodded absently as she stared at her laptop monitor.

Susan considered her next words. Maybe it would be better to address the elephant in the room though it was probably her guilt talking. "Are you questioning making me a partner?"

"What?" Harri's head jerked up. "No! What makes you think that?"

"You don't seem to trust me to handle things," Susan said. Maybe Harri shouldn't trust her. She didn't like the fact Nesmith and Consuelo didn't want Harri to know about Trubble's death. Well, possible death. Or the fact that Harri might once again be someone's target.

A wry smile crossed Harri's face. "Everyone in the building will tell you I'm a control freak. You're doing a fabulous job of handling the bankruptcy trustee for Dewey and

Cheatham in the lawsuit against Mother Defiant. I'm sorry I've been so self-involved lately and not giving you enough kudos for that."

Susan's face heated. She hated showing her emotions to the world, and she hated she cared so much about Harri's opinion of her. No, it wasn't just Harri's opinion. She hated she cared about what everyone in the Lechuza Building thought of her. She never cared what people thought of her before she joined this firm.

"I haven't gotten him to drop the damn lawsuit yet."

"You will." Harri leaned her elbows on her desk. "The trustee's hoping Mother Defiant will settle. It's the only way he'll get any money for the creditors."

"Except she's just as much as a creditor since the bastards at Dewey and Cheatham embezzled most of her money." Susan cleared her throat. "However, I wasn't looking for a pat on the back. You threw a lot of stuff at Aisha, and she barely has her bags unpacked. It's shit I could handle."

Harri sighed and leaned back against her chair. "I know. Again, it's nothing you've done or haven't done. It's the stereotypical 'it's not you, it's me'. Travis said the same thing to me last Friday."

Travis Beckham had been a junior partner at Dewey and Cheatham before the rival law firm's collapse. But after a thorough check, the partners found out he had been just as much a victim as most of the staff and clients at Dewey and Cheatham. He finagled his refusal to kill Harri on Howard

Dewey's order into an associate position at Winters and Franklin. But he was turning into a damn good asset.

"You have valid reasons to be concerned about him," Susan replied. "But I left Dewey and Cheatham nearly fifteen years ago. Am I still in the hole because of them?"

"That's not what I meant." Harri sighed. "In case you haven't noticed, I have serious trust issues. It wouldn't matter who you and Travis worked for or with before now. I kind of depend on Aisha as my barometer for when I'm acting stupid.

"What I'm really trying to say is please don't leave. I will do my damnedest to dump a whole lot more work on you. In fact, if you want to deal with Captain Terrific while Aisha is in Paris, he's all yours."

"That depends." Susan grinned. "Do I need to check him into rehab again?"

"No, he's got a new endorsement for a whitening toothpaste."

"Ah, so I get the boring shit."

"No, you said you wanted more work."

Susan raised her right eyebrow.

"Okay, I fell asleep three times trying to read the contract last night," Harri admitted. "And that was with two cups of coffee."

Susan frowned as she accepted the file from Harri. "You sure your husband didn't substitute decaf for your full octane brew?" The issue of Harri's caffeine habit had been a source of bickering before she and Tim tied the knot.

Harri grinned. "I'm sure. I stole some of Aisha's."

"She's left coffee in her loft while she's gone for a year?"

"She left it for me. Because as you pointed out, my husband is trying to decaffeinate me."

"Your couple issues are more than I can handle on a Monday morning." Susan stood and grabbed her mug of Irish breakfast tea. "If there's nothing else?"

"How about we have lunch tomorrow?" Harri waved at her desk. "Unfortunately, I need to deal with the family court today."

"Sure." Susan nodded and left before she let something slip.

She walked back to her own office and plopped into her office chair. What was worse? Not telling Harri someone may be planning to kill her? Or the tiny green worms of envy crawling through her brain? It wasn't Aisha's fault she was living the dream Susan had planned and saved for over the last sixteen years.

When the hell had her life become so complicated?

When she accepted Harri and Aisha's original job offer, the tiny voice in the back of her mind said.

It seemed like such a good idea at the time. Mom had been having some health issues. Dad couldn't handle everything by himself. And Tracy had her own kids who needed her full-time attention. Settling down in Canyon Pointe again seemed like the best solution for the entire Kennedy clan. What she hadn't planned on was government conspiracies, crazed supervillains trying to kill her, or actually caring about the people she worked with.

She flipped open the folder with Captain Terrific's endorsement contract and started reading. It was pretty standard verbiage with a clause regarding the superhero's past drug addiction problems. But the contract was small potatoes. Maybe Harri didn't trust her after all.

Except Harri had confided to both her and Aisha about the weird list of names she'd found in her grandmother's storage unit. Was that the real reason Nesmith and Consuelo pulled her in? What if they knew about the list and wanted Susan to get it for them?

Or should she tell Harri that the list might be the kids Eagle Forever had tried to hide from the government?

The intercom buzzed, throwing her out of her bizarre thoughts. "Yes?"

"Qiang is on line 2 for you," Patty said.

"Thanks." Susan lifted the receiver and pressed the appropriate button. "Hey, Qiang."

"Are you free for lunch?"

"Sure. What did you have in mind?"

"There's a taco truck at the empty lot on the corner of Ninth and MLK. Can you meet me there at one?"

A suspicion shivered its way up Susan's spine. "Is this about yesterday?"

Qiang sighed. "Yeah."

Susan knew she couldn't ask more. The firm's IT guru Arthur Drallhickey recorded every call coming into and out of the law firm. In the past, it had saved lives. But now?

She hated the feeling she was in the middle of a deal she couldn't get out of.

"All right. One p.m. at 9th and MLK," she said.

The line abruptly died. Sometimes, Susan wondered if Qiang's son wasn't the only one who was on the spectrum. She glanced at the clock on her computer monitor. She had nearly three hours to kill so she might as well start with the Captain Terrific contract.

And maybe in the process, she'd find a clue as to what she should do about the secrets she kept and where her loyalties truly lay.

CHAPTER 6

Harri strode into Family Court Number Four at one-thirty p.m. The bailiff eyed her, so she flashed him a smile. This was the second time in her life she was an attorney in a family court. All the other times, she'd been the kid the adults were fighting over.

Two groups of people sat on opposite sides of the gallery, whispering to each other while eyeing the other group. But it was the older man talking to Cathy who drew Harri's attention. Either Special Agent Nesmith of the National Superhero Bureau had several suits in the exact same color and style, or he wore the same navy suit every time she saw him.

"Good afternoon, Cathy," Harri said warmly as she approached the court clerk's desk. She let her tone drop several degrees colder before she said, "Agent Nesmith."

"Ms. Winters." From the twinkle in his blue eyes, he was more amused than perturbed by her behavior. He'd been doing his best to insinuate himself with her firm, but trust of any federal authority, much less the NSB, didn't come easily with her. Not after Rey's abduction and Steve's brainwashing.

Harri turned back to Cathy. "Will Judge Shriver allow me to talk to my client prior to the hearing?"

She nodded. "He's in chambers with the judge. Go on back."

Harri glanced behind her. That explained the folks on separate sides of the gallery. She headed for the door behind Cathy's desk. Past the courtroom door, she took a left and knocked on the partly open door to Judge Shriver's inner sanctum.

"Come in."

Harri pushed the door open a little wider and entered. "Harri Winters, attorney ad litem for Diego Murphy."

Judge Shriver was roughly ten years older than Harri, but she looked younger. Her dark hair was cut in a chin-length bob, and she wore just enough makeup to emphasize her big brown eyes and full lips. She waved at the teenager slumped in the judge's visitor chair, who had opened his eyes at his name.

"Your client, counselor."

The kid's sullen expression turned a little bit brighter. "I really get my own attorney?"

"Yes, Mr. Murphy," Judge Shriver replied.

"Is there someplace he and I can talk?" Harri asked.

"There's a mediation room three doors to your left." The judge pointed with her pen. "It should be unlocked."

"Thank you, Your Honor." Harri nodded. "Mr. Murphy, let's get to know each other."

The kid stood, but she recognized his defeated expression. Too many adults who were supposed to take care of her had screwed her over as well. But he did trudge after her as she strode down the hall to the room the judge had indicated.

Once inside the mediation room, he flung himself into one of the wheeled chairs and twirled around in it. Yep, teen attitude all the way around.

"What do you want, Mr. Murphy?"

He stopped twirling. "Aren't you supposed to pretend you're my friend?"

"Nope, I'm your attorney ad litem assigned by the court. Not to mention, we've just met." Harri placed her bag on the table and sat down across from her client. "So, what is it you want?"

"Why do you care?"

She leaned back in her chair. "Who says I do?"

"Then why are you here?"

"Because I don't like the idea of locking up kids when they haven't done anything wrong."

Diego smirked. "But I'm dangerous."

"Dangerous for wanting to be normal?"

He held up his hand, and flames danced along his open palm. "All they want is this. No one cares about me."

Now, she was getting somewhere. "Who wants your powers?"

"Mom and Dad don't want me. They just want me to suit up for the money." He turned and stared out the window. "And everyone knows what happens to the kids deemed too dangerous to be in public."

Her heart pounded. This could have easily been Rey and Steve at the same age. The twins were damn lucky they had people who cared. Too bad Rey was in Europe. And Steve had his adoptive parents' silver spoon in his mouth so Diego wouldn't listen to him. But there was one other super she knew who grew up in the system like she did, and maybe, just maybe, Shadowstar could get through to Diego.

"What if I said there was a third door?" She leaned her elbows on the table. "Would you take it?"

He looked at her suspiciously. "That depends. What's it going to cost me?"

Damn, this kid was smart. Not Francisco's genius smart. More like Javier's street smart. And Miguel's third born would accept Diego for himself. Just like Javier did with Qiang's son Connor.

She shrugged. "All I ask is you keep up with your classes. You'd have your own bedroom and bath I will require you keep clean. And most important of all, don't set my loft on fire."

Diego eyed her, but his suspicion gave way to surprise. "Do you have kids?"

"Not me, but there's a couple of other families that live in our building."

"Where's your place located?"

"The Canyon Block."

Instead of the derisive expression she half-expected, his eyes widened. "The north side where the Ghost Owl patrols?"

"Yes." She smiled. "In fact, the Ghost Owl is a client."

Diego turned toward the window again. When he turned back, he wore a dejected look.

"My parents won't be happy if I go live with you."

"It sounds to me like your parents aren't going to be happy no matter what you decide." Harri exhaled before she added, "Let me guess. Your parents' arguments grew a lot worse once they found out you're a super."

He nodded. That explained why both the judge and Special Agent Nesmith insisted she take this case. Poor kid. How exactly did his parents plan to pull off Diego becoming a superhero? Gaslight him for the next five years so he gave them all the money when he changed his NSB registration?

"There's a reason you can't become a superhero until you turn eighteen," she said. "You can't legally sign your contracts."

"Mom said she and Dad could sign for me."

"And anyone who would accept a parent's signature for a super kid knows damn well both they and the parents could spend a very long time in prison. There's laws to protect minors like you for a reason."

"What happens if my mom and dad get back together? Will I have to live with them again?"

Harri sighed. "I don't know. It depends on whether Judge Shriver believes they've truly reconciled. There's a lot of other factors she will take into account, including what you think."

He sunk further down in his seat. "If I tell the truth, they'll just say I'm lying."

Harri's internal alarm went off. "Have they hurt you or tried to, Diego?"

"They used to threaten to kick me out of the house all the time."

"Bu not since your powers kicked on, right?"

He shook his head.

No wonder he didn't trust his parents. Out of all the shitty things her dad did, he and the stepmonster never threatened to kick her out of the house. But then, they would have had to be sober to remember she was there most of the time.

"So to be clear, you don't want to live with either your mom or your dad at the moment. Right?"

Diego shook his head again.

"All right." Harri stood. "Let's go see what Judge Shriver says."

"W-will she make me go home with one of them?" He shook so hard he could barely stand.

"I can't guarantee anything, but I'll do my best to make sure the judge hears your side of the story, Mr. Murphy."

"Call me Diego," he murmured.

"Then I'm Harri." She smiled.

As they walked toward the courtroom, she prayed Judge Shriver wouldn't do anything stupid. This kid needed some stability and responsible adults who gave a shit about him. And definitely not the type of stability the federal government offered. The federal facility for super juveniles wasn't much better than Mauvaises, the super-max prison for supervillians.

CHAPTER 7

Susan parked her car on Ninth Street, fed the meter, and headed for the intersection with MLK Drive. While she had texted Qiang she would be fifteen minutes late after getting caught on a call, traffic hadn't cooperated. Now, it was twenty-five after one. If there was one thing that was her ultimate pet peeve, it was when anyone, including herself, was late.

Qiang stood near the taco truck, looking every bit like a suburban mom in her matching sweater and skirt set, pumps, and sunglasses. But instead of being impatient, she wore a huge grin.

"Let me guess," she said. "It was Vicki on the phone."

"You know I can neither confirm nor deny any client conversations." Susan grinned back. Victoria "Vicki" Danvers AKA Silver Shield had been in panic mode over an upcoming ad shoot. To the point, she wanted a whole makeover. Costume, hair, the works.

"I know damn well that woman cannot stop talking to save her life." Qiang chuckled.

It was nice to see her in a good mood. Usually, she was quite taciturn unless she was throwing insults at Harri. Maybe dating Steve had loosened her up a bit.

"Lunch first because I'm starving, then gossip," Susan said.

Once they had their meals and drinks, Qiang led the way to Allen George Memorial Park diagonally across from the empty lot. Other than a few parents with toddlers at the playground, the park was fairly empty.

The two women claimed an unoccupied picnic bench and sat. Susan unwrapped her first taco and took a bite when Qiang blurted, "I don't like keeping secrets, especially from Harri."

Susan chewed and swallowed the mouthful, but the corn shell and beef burned their way down her esophagus. "Neither do I. But both Consuelo and Nesmith are right. Harri would go off half-cocked. It's the way she's built. And since when do you give a shit about Harri's feelings?"

"Since Steve pointed out I was letting my own guilt and embarrassment stand in the way," Qiang admitted.

That made sense. Seismic Shift had threatened to kill Qiang's son and parents two years ago if she didn't kill Harri. Except Harri had shocked everyone when she disabled Qiang with an antique, and very expensive, lead crystal vase full of roses and water Tim had given Harri.

"I've been second-guessing their request, too." Susan looked around them, but there was no one near by. "How's

Tim going to do his job as the firm's chief of security if he's not aware of the threat?"

"Except he'd tell Harri because she's his wife." Qiang stared at her unwrapped, uneaten taco for a moment. "What if another super moves into the Lechuza Building?"

"You've been pretty adamant you were not joining our little commune," Susan teased.

The super snorted. "My reasoning still stands. I mean what if another super sublets Aisha and Rey's loft for the rest of the time they're in Paris?"

"Aisha offered to let Molly housesit while they were gone."

"But . . ." Qiang raised an eyebrow.

"Part of the reason she said no was because she didn't want to leave her grandmother totally alone. Kerry and her girlfriend have been spending nights at the girlfriend's place when Kerry isn't on patrol." Susan shrugged. "On the other side, Molly was seriously miffed Rey and Aisha insisted she go back to school instead of accompanying them to Europe."

"She needs to make a life for herself." Qiang sipped her diet soda. "Her grandmother isn't going to be around forever, and she can't keep riding on Kerry's coattails."

Qiang had a point. Kerry was the more dominant of the twin girls. When Molly did think for herself, it was usually some stunt design to piss off her grandmother, the retired superhero the rest of the world knew as Rue Liberty. But Kerry was in a serious relationship now, and it seemed like Molly wasn't sure what to do with herself.

Susan sighed. "You know that, and I know that, but we each have roughly twenty years on the kid."

"True." A sly smile crossed Qiang's face. "The agents in charge didn't say I couldn't bring another super into the loop though."

"So you're going to talk Molly into moving to the Lechuza Building anyway?" Susan reached into the bag for her second taco.

"You got a better idea?"

"Tell Harri that Trubble is dead."

"Except we don't know for sure he is yet," Qiang pointed out. "It's still going to take a week or two for the genetic testing to get back to the FBI office from their lab in D.C., and that's assuming it's accurate."

"You think Trubble may have faked his death?"

"I wouldn't put it past him or whoever ordered Miss Purrception to kidnap him to fake his demise. You know damn well she didn't make that decision on her own. She would have killed him and made sure the body was never found."

Susan chewed a bite of her taco while she contemplated Qiang's analysis. If Trubble had escaped from his captors like Aisha suspected and he had any sense, faking his death would keep his captors off his ass. At least long enough for him to hide somewhere like Mal Paraíso, an island owned by a cabal of supervillains. Trubble was technically considered one of them after his trial last year.

On the other hand, if Miss Purrception's employers had gotten everything they wanted out of Trubble, there was simply no sense in keeping him alive.

"The kidnappers have had him for what? About six months," Susan said. "Why fake his death now?"

Qiang shrugged. "You got me. I'm not a supervillain, and I don't know why they would want supers who have been in hiding for the last fifty to sixty years. If they are still alive, they're eligible for AARP membership. What does anyone want with them? Hell, Judge Inunza didn't even have his grandfather's powers, and Trubble was searching for him anyway."

"I agree with you." Susan wiped her fingers on a napkin. "None of this makes any sense."

"We don't have all the pieces." Qiang gestured with the fresh taco she pulled out of her own bag. "Unless—"

"We tell Harri what's going on." The idea left a sour taste that had nothing to do with the delicious street tacos. While Susan sympathized with the agents not wanting Harri to do something Harri-like and blow up their investigation, she also had a duty to her law partner. Besides it would ease Harri's mind to know her grandmother worked to protect those kids, not kidnap them for the government's use. Assuming Nesmith and Consuelo were right about Mrs. Winters funding Eagle Forever's Underground Railroad.

"I'll follow your lead on this one," Qiang said. "You know the legal ramifications better than I do."

"I hate to tell you this, but the government holds superheroes to as high a standard as they hold attorneys."

"But you don't represent the government."

"No, I don't." Susan frowned as she considered the problem. "What if Consuelo and Nesmith think Harri does have documentation from her grandmother and they're hoping we do tell her?"

Blood drained from Qiang's face. "That means they were behind Trubble's abduction to begin with."

Susan set her taco on the table. Her appetite had disappeared with the super's conclusion. "Unless they're in the dark as much as we are. They didn't have to tell us about the body."

"The only reason they did is because they didn't have Aisha here to manipulate." Resentment laced Qiang's voice. "And you know damn well Aisha would have told Harri about the body in the desert regardless of what any federal agent said."

Susan stared at her half-eaten taco. Qiang was right. Aisha didn't keep secrets from her partners. Susan looked up at Qiang. "I'll tell Harri when she gets back from court, but I may need you to help me hold her down so she doesn't do anything stupid."

The super grinned. "It would be my pleasure."

CHAPTER 8

Harri walked into the courtroom, Diego on her heels. Special Agent Nesmith was still there, as she expected. He perched on a chair next to the bailiff.

Lisa Ashcraft sat with the couple on the left side of the gallery. A surprised expression that had nothing to do with Lisa's botoxed forehead spread across the other attorney's face. Lisa murmured something to the couple and motioned she would by right back.

When Harri had seen Lisa was the husband's attorney on the paperwork Cathy had e-mailed to her, her appointment as ad litem made even more sense than Nesmith's recommendation. Even though Harri was on friendly terms with Lisa, she wouldn't back down to Lisa's high-pressure tactics.

While Lisa approached, Harri bent close to Diego's ear. "Have a seat in the jury box while I talk to your parents' attorneys."

The kid didn't say a word, but he did flop in one of the seats she indicated.

One of the men on the other side of the gallery rose when he noticed Lisa walking toward Harri. From the expensive, tailored suit and equally expensive haircut, she would lay a week's worth of margaritas at La Churro's he worked for Bryson Gaither. With the demise of Dewey and Cheatham, Bryson Gaither was now Canyon Pointe's largest law firm.

"Are you switching practice specialties, Harri?" Lisa wore her normal smile, which meant she didn't hold a grudge about their last encounter. Maybe she learned her lesson about representing lying murderous assholes like Patty's ex-boyfriend Cade Wilson, AKA Black Death.

"Just doing my pro bono hours as attorney ad litem for the family courts." Harri smiled in return. "It was my partners' and staff's suggestion to keep me from messing in their lives."

"How is Grace doing?" Lisa had to get in one dig after losing to Harri.

"My goddaughter is doing great. She's walking and attempting to talk."

The man in the suit joined them and flashed a grin that could be only acquired through some very expensive dental work. "I'm Brick Montgomery, and you are?" He stuck out his right palm.

"Harri Winters." She shook his hand. "Attorney ad litem for your client's son Diego."

"Harri . . . Winters?" His blinding white smile faltered. "Of Winters and Franklin?"

"That's me."

"But this is a family law matter," he stammered.

Lisa rolled her eyes.

"With a minor who's a super," Harri said. "Or does your client want her son to end up in a NSB facility?"

"Of course, she doesn't," Montgomery snapped.

"Good. That will make this matter easier for all parties concerned."

"You can't sign a minor to representation as a super." Montgomery glared at her and straightened to a full six feet. She glanced at his shoes. With lifts, of course.

"Have you told your client Diego can't don a cape until his turns eighteen? Because according to my client, she wants to put him to work."

Before Montgomery could respond, the bailiff called out, "All rise."

"I'm not finished with you," the lawyer hissed at Harri.

Lisa rolled her eyes to say, "Can you believe what I'm dealing with?"

Everyone on the courtroom who wasn't already standing got to their feet.

Everyone except Diego.

Harri glared at him. He made a sour face, but he stood just before Judge Shriver walked into the courtroom.

"Family Court Number Four is in session. Judge Felicity Shriver presiding," the bailiff finished.

She climbed the two steps to her chair and sat. "Be seated."

Lisa and Montgomery retreated to the two lawyers' tables and took their chairs. Harri stepped into the jury box and sat next to Diego.

The judge put on her reading glasses. "This is a hearing for temporary physical custody of the minor Diego Murphy in the matter of Murphy v. Murphy," she intoned before she looked up. "Ms. Ashcraft?"

Lisa stood. "Your Honor, my client maintains his son Diego has been living with him since his separation from Mrs. Murphy. There's no reason why Diego shouldn't continue to do so."

The woman behind Montgomery jumped to her feet. "What about him setting fire to the school? I'm the one that got dragged out of work to pick him up!"

Harri looked at Diego who shrugged and muttered, "It was one paper airplane a jerk in science threw at me."

There was definitely more to the story than that. If he was being bullied in addition to his parents splitting and learning he had superpowers, no wonder he had an attitude. That was an awful lot for one thirteen-year-old to digest.

"Mrs. Murphy, either sit down and be quiet, or I'll hold you in contempt," Judge Shriver said.

The man with Mrs. Murphy looked similar enough he could be her brother. He tugged her arm a couple of times before she resumed her seat.

"Continue, counselor." The judge motioned for Lisa to proceed.

"Even though the middle school has been instructed several times to call my client in regards to Diego, they refuse to do so." Lisa frowned. "My client regrets the vice-principal decided to call Mrs. Murphy that day. However, it was a minor incident with a piece of paper. Diego did not, as she said, set the entire school on fire."

Judge Shriver took off her glasses and regarded Mr. Murphy. "And how does you client plan to deal with his son's pyrokinetic abilities?"

Nesmith's attention perked as that question.

"He's—" Lisa started.

"If you don't mind, counselor, I'd like to hear directly from your client." The judge stared the man on Lisa's side the room.

Lisa motioned for her client to stand. He cleared his throat.

"I've bought six fire extinguishers, one for each room of the house plus one for the garage. I've also tried to get Diego into anger management therapy, but Karla refuses to agree to it."

Karla Murphy surged to her feet once again, but the man accompanying her yanked her back down to the bench. Hard. They whispered furiously at each other while her soon-to-be ex-husband continued his recitation.

"I've tried to spend as much time with Diego as I can,

and I've followed the court's guidelines about managing a difficult situation like a divorce—"

Both Diego and his mother snorted derisively.

"—but I don't want my son to end up in a government facility just because he's different, Your Honor."

"Do you have anything to add, counselor?"

"If you decide Diego shouldn't be with his father, we ask that Harri Winters becomes Diego's temporary guardian ad litem in addition to his attorney ad litem."

Well, that was a tactic out of left field, even for Lisa.

CHAPTER 9

A thread of excitement wiggled its way through Aisha while she paid the taxi driver and exited the cab. She slung her overnight bag over her shoulder and headed into the train station. It was her first night away from Mitch, except for the couple of nights her parents had watched him. It was her first night away from Rey since he'd come home to her after Professor Paranoia had kidnapped him. However, this trip was a normal adventure. She needed a little more normal in her life.

Though, it had been a little surprising when Rey suggested she take a train this evening and spend the night in London so she would be fresh for her meeting in the morning. It had been more surprising Harri didn't argue about her taking the lead on the possible deal with Amblehurst, Mintegue, and Trott.

Granted, her best friend may have exploded after she got off the phone. Aisha really hoped that wasn't the case. They couldn't afford for Susan to leave the firm over Harri's temper tantrums. Not if things went as Aisha hoped in tomorrow's meeting.

She boarded the train and found her seat. The chair was a heck of a lot more comfortable than the one on the flight from the States. Too bad every time rail legislation came up in the U.S., it got shot down. Maybe if more Americans experienced the European rail system, their minds would be changed. Europe definitely knew how to travel in style.

The car was only half full when the train pulled away from the station. The conductor announced their projected arrival time in London in both French and English. A little over two hours. What she wouldn't give for a ride like this to Hermanville rather flying in a cramped commuter plane or driving through the desert.

Aisha retrieved her tablet from the side pocket of her soft-sided briefcase and leaned back in the cushy seat. This was the first evening totally by herself since Mitch was born. She'd have plenty of time to review her notes in the morning. Tonight, she had two hours to indulge in a steamy romance, something she always felt weird about given Rey's library of literary classics in the loft.

She was just past the hero and heroine's initial meeting in the lobby of a D.C. hotel when a woman screamed. Someone shouted in French, "Everyone on the floor!"

Aisha looked up to find a masked man standing by the open door to the rest of the train at the front of the car. Medium height. Dressed all in black. Worse, he held a military-style assault rifle. The female passenger four rows in front of Aisha and on the opposite side of the car kept screaming.

The masked man fired a couple of rounds into the ceiling. Aisha dropped her tablet and slapped her hands over her ears at the deafening noise in such a small area made mostly of metal. She lowered herself to the floor and peered through the space between the two seats in front of her.

"Shut up!" The masked gunman pointed his weapon at the screaming woman. "Shut up, or I'll kill you!"

"Wait!" Aisha knelt on the floor and held up her hands. The masked man swung his barrel to point it at her. "Let her come back to me. I'll keep her shut." She winced at her messed up French, but at least, the gunman hadn't shot her.

Not that it would kill her, but the bullet could ricochet off her skin and hurt someone else.

"American." The gunman turned her nationality into a slur. Too bad she didn't have the British accent Harri always manifested when she spoke Spanish. "Think you're a hero?"

"N-n-no." Aisha forced herself to stutter. "You're not going to get what you want if you start killing prisoners before you make your demands to your government."

"Who says the idiots in Paris represent me?" he sneered. "Get up here." He motioned with his rifle.

Aisha slipped her tablet into her case, slung it over her shoulder, and started to rise.

"No!" he barked. "Leave the bags!"

She slipped into English. "Okayokayokay. Don't shoot. Don't shoot." She dropped her case and her overnight bag on her seat.

"Get up here!" he yelled in French.

She didn't have to act. Her entire body shook as she walked to where the other woman had been reduced to whimpering. The Garcia-Franklins were legally restricted from any superheroics while in France. If she could contact Lightstreak or Raindrop—

Another masked man appeared in the doorway to the next car forward. His rifle was slung over his shoulder, and he held a black cloth bag. "Give me your phones!"

So much for that bright idea.

Aisha slowly pulled her phone from her pocket and dropped it into the second gunman's bag. She turned back to the quivering woman pressed against the window seat. Her pale skin showed no color other than her huge blue eyes. Her dark hair had a few silver threads, but she probably wasn't much older than Aisha.

"Give me your phone," she said in French.

The woman reached into her purse, but she was shaking so bad when she removed her phone, it slipped from her fingers.

"Bitch!"

Another shot from the rifle sent stabbing pain through Aisha's ears. Scarlet blossomed on the shoulder of the woman's cream cardigan. She started screaming again.

"Fuck up again, and I'll make the next shot count," the first gunman snarled. "Get the phone!" He pointed his rifle at Aisha.

She crouched, picked up the phone, and dropped it in the second gunman's bag. The man in the seat across the aisle cowered behind his solid aluminum briefcase as he dropped his phone in the black bag. Aisha couldn't blame him.

"Shut her up, or I'll shut her up permanently," the first gunman ordered.

"Let me get my carryon," she replied. "I can use my clothes to stop her bleeding, and I have a bottle of painkillers."

The second gunman whispered something to his partner in a language Aisha didn't recognize.

"Get your bags." The first gunman waved his rifle at her seat.

She didn't give him a chance to change his mind. It was all she could do to move at normal human speed but still hurry without unnerving the two gunmen. She retrieved her carryon and briefcase and returned to the injured woman, whose screams had been reduced to loud, gulping sobs.

The first gunman watched her while his partner collected the phones from the rest of the passengers in the car. She pulled out the cotton knit t-shirt and shorts she wore as pajamas. It took a little fishing around to find the bottle of acetaminophen in the bottom of the bag. She'd found out the hard way that though she may be damn near indestructible, she still felt the pain.

The small roll of duct tape was a lot easier to find. It scared her how many of Tim's weird habits she'd picked up over the last couple of years.

Aisha tried not to wince at the amount of blood soaking the other woman's sweater. "I'm going to take off your clothes," she murmured in French.

Despite the other woman's terror, a ghost of a smile floated across her face. "You mean my cardigan?"

"I apologize." Aisha smiled. "French isn't even one of my first three languages."

"I think we'll manage." The woman bit her lower lip to keep from screaming again as Aisha peeled the blood-soaked sleeve back from her wounded shoulder.

"What's your name?" Aisha tried not to make faces. She needed to keep the other woman calm. The coppery scent of the blood was making her nauseated though, and throwing up on the lady would not help the situation.

"Eloise."

"Hello, Eloise. I'm Aisha. Can you fold forward so I can see your back?"

Eloise leaned forward. No exit wound. There was an awful lot of blood for a single entry.

Aisha folded her t-shirt into a thick pad and pressed it against the gunshot wound. Eloise groaned and bit her lip hard enough that it also bled.

"Eloise, I need you to hold my shirt in place while I stick it." Aisha held up the roll of silver tape.

The woman nodded and placed her hand over the wad of cotton t-shirt. Her entire body shook as Aisha peeled the cardigan off and taped the pad in place. Aisha shook out four capsules for Eloise and unscrewed the cap on the bottle of water in Eloise's bag.

Eloise choked down the pills with some water. Tears ran down her face when she handed the bottle back to Aisha.

"Can I sit back now?"

Aisha nodded. However, she didn't like how Eloise's teeth chattered. Shock was a real possibility. She stood to remove her jacket.

"What do you think you're doing?" The first gunman jabbed her with the end of his barrel.

"I'm taking off my coat. She is going into-into—" Aisha struggled to find the correct French word.

"Shock," Eloise supplied. "A blanket would be better. I don't want to ruin your jacket."

"Get the fucking blankets!" The first gunman waved his rifle. "Then you both need to sit down and shut the fuck up if you want to live!"

Aisha carefully and slowly moved to the compartment she'd seen the conductor open to retrieve napping paraphernalia for a little boy in the car. She retrieved two of the lavender-scented navy blankets and two pillows. It was an ugly thought, but she may need the fluff from a pillow to pack

Eloise's wound if her makeshift pressure pad didn't stop the bleeding.

Thankfully, the first gunman said nothing more as Aisha helped Eloise to recline her seat and prop up her feet on her own carryon case. While she made the injured woman comfortable, the second gunman entered the car behind theirs.

Aisha leaned back in the seat next to Eloise. The train hadn't altered its velocity one bit. Did that mean the engineer had no clue of what was happening? Or did these asshats control the train? And what was their endgame?

She hated feeling helpless, but until she had more information, she needed to play the waiting game. No matter how much it sucked.

CHAPTER 10

Unfortunately, Susan had another pile of shit dumped on her when she returned to her office from lunch. She stared at the three men who sat on the other side of her desk. "You are all insane. Why are you involving me in this?"

"Because I need to get into Dewey and Cheatham without breaking in." Harri's husband Tim Canyon was a certified genius who, on paper, was Winters and Franklin's head of security. He'd also been the vigilante Jatz'om Kuh, the original Ghost Owl.

Or was until the man sitting on his right forced his retirement. Steve Connor was technically a law student and an intern at the law firm. He was also Rey's twin brother and a super in his own right. Currently, he donned the uniforms of Rey's alter ego Black Falcon and Aisha's alter ego the new Ghost Owl while the Garcia-Franklin family was in Paris. The firm couldn't afford for the public to even suspect the two supers were gone at the same time as Rey and Aisha.

However, the men's biological mother had separated them

at birth to protect them from her own enemies. Before the twins learned about each other, Steve had been kidnapped and brainwashed by Professor Paranoia. The kid had nearly killed Tim in the supervillain's efforts to destroy the reputation of Rey's first superhero persona, Captain Justice.

Like Susan and Aisha, Travis Beckham was a refugee from Dewey and Cheatham. Unlike Susan and Aisha, it took Howard Dewey demanding Travis shoot Harri before the attorney realized how corrupt the bankrupt firm was.

But Harri had a thing about adopting strays, and Travis was one in a long line.

For that matter, so was Susan herself.

That realization sent a surge of guilt through her gut, disturbing the lump of tacos she'd eaten.

"You're not an attorney, you're not an intern, and you're not a paralegal." Susan shook her head. "I can't justify taking you with me to the discovery meeting tomorrow. And if you get caught, I'm the one who will lose their license."

"Tim, if you tell me what to look for, I can get it for you," Travis said.

"And you know damn well if you get caught, we both lose our licenses," Susan snapped. "And after everything you went through at Dewey and Cheatham, why are you so eager to follow their illicit footsteps?"

"That's the reason you should take me with you tomorrow," Steve said. "With my superspeed, I can—"

"No!" Susan glared at him. "Crap like that is why there's so many freakin' laws governing super behavior."

"Susan, can we speak alone for the moment?" Tim asked.

"You're not going to change my mind."

"But I also don't want anyone to lose their law license." He looked at Steve. "Or the potential of obtaining one."

"Fine," she growled. "I'll give you one minute, but I'm still planning to take Bethany with me because she's the only one not proposing to do illegal shit."

Travis and Steve exchanged looks, but they stood without a word and left her office. Steve even gently pulled her door shut.

"That doesn't mean you can stand outside my office and listen with your damn superhearing, Steve," she said.

Two shadows passed by the frosted glass in the direction of the guys' own offices.

Tim snickered. "You've picked up on everyone's peccadillos quite nicely."

"No, you're all so fucking predictable. I honestly don't get how the bad guys aren't kicking your asses," she snapped. "Fifty-five seconds."

"Someone did a search on one of the names from Harri's list."

Blood roared in Susan's ears. "When?"

"A couple of weeks ago." Tim drummed his fingers against the arm of his chair. "Arthur traced the search and correlated with subsequent searches in the NSB database. The person in question was a fifteen-year-old who was turned over to the government by his own parents nearly seventy years ago. He was killed in a training accident at the NSB juvenile facility."

Susan leaned back in her chair. "If he died, why give him an alternate identity?"

"The second identity was created before the boy was killed." The drumming of Tim's fingers stopped. "Someone planned to liberate him from NSB custody."

"And the who goes back to Mrs. Winters?"

Tim nodded.

"But why, unless she was doing it for Trubble?"

Tim shrugged. "Unless it was for our mysterious third party who had Miss Purrception kidnap Trubble."

Part of Susan wanted to walk away from Winters and Franklin. Her specialty was superhero law, not espionage and escaping from murderers and battling supervillains. Nesmith and Consuelo were wrong. Harri needed to know what the agents had found in the desert.

"Is Harri back from court yet?"

"Not yet." Tim frowned. "Why?"

"Because I only want to tell this story once." Or for that matter, get lectured only once concerning yesterday's meeting with the FBI and the NSB.

CHAPTER 11

<hr>

Harri held her breath when Brick Montgomery jumped to his feet. "I object!"

"May I ask why the change in your motion without notice to the opposing party, Ms. Ashcraft?" Judge Shriver didn't look one bit happy about Lisa's stunt, but Harri wasn't about to draw the judge's displeasure in her direction.

Not to mention, Harri had the distinct impression earlier Lisa hadn't known Harri had been assigned as attorney ad litem. Was Lisa covering up the fact she wasn't paying attention to her own client's case? If so, that wasn't like her at all.

"My client's main concern is the safety and welfare of Diego," Lisa stated. "Given the circumstances, if he does not have physical custody of his son, he would prefer Ms. Winters have custody rather than his wife or, no offense to Special Agent Nesmith, the NSB."

The corners of Nesmith's mouth twitched, but he remained silent and still.

"That doesn't answer my question, counselor."

Harri got the definite impression the judge was about to throw the contempt book at Lisa if she didn't do some quick thinking.

"If Mr. Montgomery objects to either my verbal motion to the court or Ms. Winters as guardian ad litem, we would be happy to reschedule this hearing for a later date. After I've served him with my written motion, of course. Diego's well-being and his classmates' safety should be the court's paramount concern."

So that was it. Lisa was worried about losing this hearing over the incident with the school.

"Your Honor, I do not agree to opposing counsel's motion." Montgomery's face flushed a brilliant red. "I want a ruling on my objection."

"I'm withholding a ruling for the moment, Mr. Montgomery," the judge said. "However, you may proceed with your statement."

The attorney didn't look one bit happy, but he didn't argue with the judge. She could just as easily slap a contempt charge on him. "Your Honor, my client's life was threatened by her husband when she left the family home—"

Mr. Murphy snorted derisively.

"—and wanted to take her son with her." Montgomery continued. "She's worried about Diego's welfare with her husband since he insists the child needs to make money to support him. She misses her only child and wants him to live with her. Since she's had to shoulder the burden of dealing with the school over Diego's behavior, she should have primary physical custody."

Mrs. Murphy jumped to her feet for a third time. "Don't I have the chance to say anything? You listened to him prattle." She jabbed her index finger in the direction of her soon-to-be ex-husband.

"I'll give you the same fifteen seconds I gave Mr. Murphy." Judge Shriver smiled. "But my warning about contempt still stands, Mrs. Murphy."

She blew a couple of her seconds by fuming and flaring her nostrils. "Brian only wants Diego because he thinks he can make money from him becoming a superhero. At least, I'd give my son the choice." She flounced back down on the bench.

Mr. Murphy turned beet red and started to stand. The woman with him whispered in his ear, and he leaned back against his bench.

What a load of crock! Harri had to dig her nails into her palms to keep from shouting a few obscenities herself. Neither of these two idiots could keep their stories straight. She'd read the report from the school vice-principal.

The vice-principal was the one who suggested anger management for Diego. She'd only called the mother when she couldn't get a hold of the father after a half hour of repeated attempts.

From the look on Nesmith's face, he knew what a bullshit story both sides were giving, too. No wonder he pushed the judge into assigning Harri as ad litem. And he probably guessed what the judge's next move would be after watching the parents in action.

Judge Shriver turned to her. "Your analysis after meeting with your client, Ms. Winters?"

Harri stood. "Given the emotional states of the parents and my client, I request I be made temporary guardian ad litem of Diego Murphy as well as attorney ad litem. In lieu of myself as guardian, there are a few supers who would agree to act as guardian for Diego if the court does not wish me to act in the capacities of both attorney and guardian ad litem. Such a break will give both parties in this case an opportunity to focus on the technical matters of the divorce without my client being caught in the middle."

The judge smiled. "Does your husband know about your request, Ms. Winters?"

"Not yet, but we've discussed adoption." Harri grinned. "This will be good practice for him."

"Wait a minute, Your Honor," Montgomery protested. "Who is Ms. Winters's husband? While we accede to the court's authority to assign Ms. Winters as guardian ad litem of Diego Murphy as well as attorney ad litem, neither my client nor Ms. Ashcraft's client are going to accept some stranger if the court hasn't cleared this man."

"Please speak for your own client, counselor" Lisa said. "We have no objection to Diego staying with Ms. Winters and her husband for the time being, Your Honor."

"I do object!" Red crawled up Montgomery's neck. "My client has a right to know who her son is living with!"

"My husband is Tim Canyon," Harri said.

It took three very long seconds for the information to register in Montgomery's brain. The blood drained from his face when it did. His mouth opened and closed twice.

On the other hand, the corner of Judge Shriver's mouth twitched. "I was a bridesmaid in Tim and Becky Canyon's wedding twenty-eight years ago. I personally trust him. And he was cleared of her murder as well as their son's. I would be very careful about what you say next in my courtroom."

Montgomery cleared his throat. "I withdraw my objection."

"All right." The judge's smile was less brittle than Lisa's. "Parties in this care are hereby ordered to mediation. And counselors, I'm not in the mood for more delays, so get it done." She slipped her glasses back on and scribbled notes in the court's file. "We'll reschedule this hearing for forty-five days from today. Cathy?"

The clerk hit a few keystrokes on her computer. "That will put us at March 6th. Is nine a.m. good?" She looked up at the three attorneys.

"Fine with me," Harri said.

"Me, too," Lisa added.

"Y-Yes," Montgomery choked out.

"Very good." The judge peered over the rims of her reading glasses. "By the way, Ms. Winters, congratulations on your recent nuptials. I'm glad to see Tim happy again. Court is dismissed."

As Judge Shriver exited her courtroom, Harri leaned closer to Diego. "Did you want to talk to your mom and dad before we go?"

He gave a slight shake of his head, but it was the pleading in his big brown eyes that got to her. She remembered giving Aisha's parents the same damn look when they asked if she wanted to come live with them. She hadn't been much older than Diego at the time.

"Go back to the judge's office with Cathy," Harri said. "I'll be back there in a few minutes."

Thankfully, Cathy picked up on the hint and escorted Diego to the back offices while she asked if he wanted a soda.

"Diego! Diego!" his mother shrieked as the kid disappeared through the door.

She may have been panicked, but Mr. Murphy had a weird mix of anger and sadness on his face.

"If you'd kept your mouth shut, he would have gone home with one of us," he snapped.

"This is all your fault!" Mrs. Murphy jabbed a finger at the woman with her husband. "If you hadn't been screwing around with that whore—"

"That's enough!" Nesmith roared.

Lisa, Montgomery, and their respective parties all jumped. The bailiff smirked.

"The judge is looking out for your son's best interest,"

he barked. "And even I'll admit, the kid's better off with Ms. Winters. An NSB facility should be the last resort for any child. But if you two don't get your shit together, that's exactly what will happen to Diego."

Nesmith gestured at Harri. "This lady has taken out supervillians all by her lonesome, and she's not a super. Don't think for one minute she can't handle your son."

He stalked toward the courtroom's main doors and grabbed a lever, but he whirled to face the parents once again. "Or you either."

When neither of them replied, the tension drained from his shoulders. "And Harri, I'm sorry I didn't say so earlier, but congratulations to you and Tim. You make a hell of a couple."

"Thanks, Wilbur." Harri smiled at the agent. Hey, if he was going to call her by her first name, she'd do the same.

Nesmith yanked the door open and departed.

Lisa and Montgomery both edged closer to Harri.

"Can our clients have some contact with Diego?" Lisa asked.

"Why don't you and Brick—" Harri had to swallow a giggle. Who the hell named their kid "Brick"? "—give me a call on Friday? With everyone's tempers on edge, we need to give the entire family a chance to cool down."

Montgomery lowered his voice. "I'll try, but I can't guarantee anything."

"Well, tell Mrs. Murphy—" Harri shot a look at Lisa.

"—and this goes for Mr. Murphy, too. If either of them just so happens to show up on Sixth Street, I will have them arrested for trespassing. Capice?"

"No problem, Harri." Lisa grinned. "And add my congratulations on your marriage to Tim. He's going to need all the luck he can get."

Harri laughed at the teasing. It was too bad she and Lisa found themselves on the opposite sides of the courtroom so often lately.

"I have to ask though," Lisa continued. "Why is that NSB agent so set on you being the ad litem?"

Even Montgomery stared at Harri intently, waiting for her answer.

"Diego's not the first super kid I've taken in." Harri smiled. "Also, Wilbur Nesmith has been with the NSB for thirty years. He knows when a super is a real danger to the public and when they just need someone to listen to them. He also knows the government taking custody of the kid isn't in anybody's best interest, but he'll do it if he has to. I hope you relay that to your clients."

Lisa nodded at Harri's not-so-subtle hint.

But Montgomery bristled. "He's underage. You can't sign him."

"Not every super I know suits up," Harri said. "And those are the folks in the best position to help Diego right now."

She pivoted and marched for the door to the back offices because if she stayed in the courtroom, she'd punch somebody. And she didn't feel like spending the night in jail.

CHAPTER 12

<hr>

After fifteen minutes, Aisha gently grasped Eloise's wrist. The woman no longer shivered, but Aisha couldn't feel her pulse and her skin was chill to the touch. She reached for the woman's neck.

When she touched Eloise's skin, the other woman's eyes opened halfway, and she smiled. "I'm still here."

"I may not be a doctor," Aisha murmured. "But I don't like the fact I can't feel your pulse in your left hand anymore."

"It may be the painkillers you gave me, but I'm rather grateful everything has gone numb."

This couldn't be good at all. Aisha looked at the first gunman. No one else had come into the car since the second gunman had left. What if the bad guys only had one person per car? If she knocked out the gunman here, she could uncouple their car from the rest of the train and fly Eloise to the closest hospital—

Aisha gritted her teeth. She only had a general clue of

where she was in France at the moment, and she had no idea where the closest hospital was. She needed to get her phone back. Or any phone. Hell, she'd settle for a couple of minutes to send Rey, or even Arthur, an e-mail or a social media direct message through her tablet.

Another thought flitted through her head, this one much more disturbing. What if each gunman was under orders to kill all the passengers in their car if anything on the train changed? If one of them was running the engine, the sensors would tell them she'd uncoupled the last cars. The second gunman and any compatriots in the cars behind them would feel the cars slow.

"What's your problem now, American?" the first gunman sneered.

"The woman you shot needs a doctor," she said as calmly as she could. "Whatever you want, you might get it a lot easier if you stop and let her off along with the little boy in the back."

"But the most vulnerable make the best hostages." His psychotic attitude sent a shiver through her. "The authorities in Europe actually worry about the weak and the helpless unlike your American government."

"Is that what this is about?" she asked. "Showing up the French government?"

"Them. The British." The gunman shrugged. "They are all the same."

"You just pointed out there's a large difference between

the European and U.S. governments, so they can't possibly be the same."

"Do you want to die?" He pointed the barrel at her once again.

"If all the governments are the same, why do you want to act like one?"

"I'm nothing like the corrupt governments!"

"Isn't this what corrupt governments do? Treat everyone like crap?" Aisha climbed out of her seat.

"Sit down," he demanded.

"Take a good look at my skin color." She raised her hands to show the backs. "I know all about getting treated like crap in my own country. My guess is you know, too, which is why you're participating in—" She waved her hands to indicate the train. "—whatever you call this. But kicking the people who are already down isn't going to change your circumstances."

The gunman hesitated for a moment. Maybe she was getting through to him. But the look in his eyes hardened, and he pointed the rifle at Eloise again. "Sit down and shut up or she dies."

Aisha slowly lowered herself back into the seat beside the wounded woman. She'd been in enough negotiations to know when to back off, but she'd made some inroads with this particular person. She just needed to bide her time.

She prayed the time she needed wouldn't come at the cost of Eloise's life.

CHAPTER 13

Once Harri and Diego were inside her ancient sedan, she tapped her phone's speed dial for Tim.

"Hey, gorgeous! Done with court? How'd the hearing go?"

"We're going to have a house guest for the next forty-five days," she said. "Diego, that's my husband Tim Canyon. Tim, this is my ward Diego Murphy."

"Hey, Diego," Tim said cheerfully.

"Hey."

At least, the kid answered him.

"We're going to make a couple of stops for some things Diego will need before we come home. I need a favor. Can you straighten up the guest bedroom and get those law files out of there?"

Tim hesitated for a split second before he said, "Sure. Where do you want them?"

"Stack them in my office in the loft for now." Harri forced a chuckle. "Just leave me a path to my desk."

"I'll do my best." Tim hesitated another second. "Uh, should I get Steve or Susan to help?"

Crap. The last thing Harri wanted was to pull Steve into her family's mess because he would definitely ask questions. At least, Susan already knew about the contents of Grandma Harri's storage unit.

"Get Susan. It may be slower, but she'll keep everything organized. Tell her I owe her a big one."

"She's an attorney, too." Tim laughed. "You need to be more specific about your offer."

"Right now tell her I'll cover the cost of a weekend in Vegas for her help."

"All right. See you when you two get home. Love you."

"Love you, too."

Harri tapped the icon to end the call and glanced at Diego in the passenger seat. She remembered the same dejected look on his face looking back at her in the mirror at the same age. The truth that your parents don't give a shit about you slaps you pretty hard, and Diego was no exception.

She started her car and backed out of the parking spot in the courts' public garage. "After we stop and get you some clothes and toiletries, you want to get something to eat?"

A muffled grunt came from his direction.

Harri may not be a parent, but she'd learned from experience that any teen who turned down food was not a good sign. She shifted the gear and headed for the garage exit.

"What's your high score on Foxstar?"

"That game is totally lame."

Well, she got a complete sentence out of him. She chalked that up to a win.

"So what's your favorite video game?"

"Bloody Jerry."

She'd heard of the popular game. Their building manager Miguel Esperanza had been adamant his older sons' could not purchase the game because of its high level of violence. At least, not until the youngest, Francisco, was a lot older. She hated to break it to Miguel that his nine-year-old son probably saw more than he should while attending college in California even with his oldest brother watching out for him.

Harri handed her parking card and cash to the booth attendant before she said, "Your parents actually let you play that?"

"Dad bought it for me last week."

She accepted her change and receipt from the attendant. "Thanks."

Harri pulled into traffic and made a left turn at the corner of Founder's Green. The last time she'd been down here at the park was when she met with Byron Trubble, the head of Corvus. Over a year and a half ago. Before he'd been sent to prison for attempting to assassinate a different family court judge. He had offered a truce between her law firm and his illegal black ops group when Professor Paranoia double-crossed Corvus and disappeared after abducting Rey.

Diego was only nine years younger than Aisha's husband.

Harri had nearly gotten Rey killed by her insistence she could make him rich by suiting up. Since then, she'd been doing her damnedest to talk Steve out of creating his own superhero persona.

And it sounded like Diego didn't want to be a hero either. Maybe she could use that.

She glanced at him as she accelerated up Main Street. "So, the parents are still at the bribing stage, huh?"

"How do you know about that?"

She could feel Diego staring at her. "Your parents aren't the only ones who don't think straight while they are fighting. My parents did something similar to get me on their side during the few times they fought about things."

"Are you going to bribe me to get me on your side?" There was total attitude in his tone, but she couldn't blame him.

"Nope."

"What's in this ad litem thing for you?" The suspicious edge in his voice let her know she'd found a sore spot.

"Not a damn thing. I'm volunteering my time and skills to the court."

"Mom says an attorney assigned by the court like you is just a way for the government to take more money from us."

"Most times the parties in a case split the fee for an ad litem, and there's a law in our state about how much it will cost. But an attorney ad litem or a guardian ad litem isn't automatically assigned in a divorce case unless there's a huge problem." Harri flipped on her left turn signal as they approached Second Street. "In my case, I'm volunteering my time for free. In legalese, it's called pro bono. Neither of your parents are paying for my time."

"Why would you do something for free?" Diego sounded genuinely puzzled.

Harri pulled into a parking spot along Second Street near the Winters flagship store and turned off the ignition before she looked at him. "Because when I was your age, a couple took me in and gave me a chance when no one else would."

"Your parents split up?"

"No."

"What happened to them?"

"My mom died in an accident when I was a few years younger than you. My dad remarried, but both he and my stepmother had a drug problem. They died in another accident."

"Did all your other family live in another state, too?" His voice quavered.

Was he worried about leaving his friends and the life he knew here in Canyon Pointe, or was he hoping to live with a relative who actually gave a shit about his existence? She needed to look into the other relatives. But it was too early to press the issue with him.

"No." She shook her head. "My only other family was my grandmother, and she died of cancer not long before my dad died."

"That sucks."

"It definitely did suck." She shrugged. "I was lucky my best friend's family took me in. But it made me want to help other people whose situations suck."

"Do you have powers?" he asked.

"Not like you." She grinned. "But I know a lot of people who do. Some suit up. Some don't."

"My parents want me to suit up. They say I could make a ton of money and take care of them."

Harri worried her tongue with her incisors to keep from saying something very inappropriate in front of her charge. She settled with, "It's nobody's decision but yours, Diego. Not mine. Not the government's. Not your parents'. Just yours. Not to mention the fact you're not allowed to become a superhero until you turn eighteen."

The kid stared out the passenger window at pedestrians on the sidewalk. "What's wrong with being normal?"

"Not a damn thing." When Diego didn't say anything else, Harri added, "Let's go get you some clothes."

They both climbed out of her car and trudged toward the department store's main entrance. Maybe she couldn't turn back the clock and prevent inflicting her bad ideas on Rey, but she could damn sure smooth the path in Diego's life.

CHAPTER 14

At the knock on Susan's office door, she yelled, "Come in!"

Time poked his head around the corner. "Can I impose on you for some help?"

Susan made a face. "Is it something illegal?"

"No." He stepped into her office and closed the door. "Harri's bringing her ad litem kid home with her. She's got to make a couple of stops first. I need help cleaning out our guest bedroom. I'd ask the interns, but you're the only one here right now who knows about the contents of Mrs. Winter's storage unit."

Susan's eyes widened. "Oh, crap! The kid does not need to see that. He'll think Harri's crazy."

"Are you sure he doesn't already?" Tim smirked.

"I meant serial killer crazy, not plain old Harri crazy."

Susan locked her computer before she followed Tim out of her office. The whole point of the law students living in the Lechuza Building and interning with the firm was to have someone to do the law office's grunt work. But the boxes of information and records wasn't something to share with the kids. Not until the partners figured out exactly what Harri's grandmother left behind and why.

Was that the real reason why Tim wanted to accompany her to her discovery session at Dewey and Cheatham? One of the original partners had been the attorney in Judge Inunza's adoption fifty years ago. Yet another potential piece of the puzzle regarding Mrs. Winters' secrets.

They reached the antique elevator. Tim shoved the double gates open, and she stepped inside the car. He started to pulled the outer gate shut when Javier Esperanza shouted, "Hold the 'vator!"

Or he tried to. The poor kid's voice cracked on the last syllable as he raced toward them.

Tim pushed the door back, and the teen slowed enough not to bounce off the elevator's back wall.

"Thanks."

"You doing anything tonight, Javi?" Tim poked the buttons for the fourth and fifth floors.

"Why? You need your ass kicked in Foxstar again?" The teen grinned.

"Harri is bringing her ad litem kid here tonight." Tim shrugged. "He's thirteen, and he'll be staying with us for a couple of months. I thought you might help him get acquainted with the building and the neighborhood."

"You know, some day I won't be here to do everybody's babysitting for them," Javi warned.

"Take it easy on him," Susan said. "His parents are splitting up, and they're fighting over him because he has powers."

"Does that mean we can't induct him in the Jatz'om Kuh League?"

"The what?" Tim's eyes narrowed as he glared at Javi.

"The Jatz'om Kuh League," the kid said. "JKL for short. That's what me and my friends call ourselves."

"You used my name for a gang?" Tim asked in disbelief.

"We're a neighborhood watch." Javi waved emphatically. "If we see anything suspicious, we let the local supers know."

"You don't have the right to use my name!"

The kid lifted his chin. "You can't sue me for violating your trademark without outing yourself."

"Except Aisha has trademarked the Ghost Owl, and she can sue you," Susan said. "Not to mention I represent the Ghost Owl on all their contracts."

"Lemme guess." Javi made a sour face. "If I don't agree to babysit Harri's new project, you'll tell my dad?"

Tim laughed. "Oh, that's way better than suing him, Susan."

"No shirts. No public signage. Nothing to draw attention to yourselves." Susan frowned at the kid. "Both Tim and Aisha have had enough people trying to kidnap or kill them over the years. Your dad will murder us—" She waved to indicate herself and Tim. "—if anything happens to you and your buddies because you're using the Jatz'om Kuh name. Got me?"

"I'll remember that next time you want us to keep an eye on who is parking on Sixth Street." Javi shot her a cheeky grin.

"You should be going to law school, not Steve," Tim muttered.

"Nah, it would be a waste of my talents," Javi replied. "Root beer and cheese balls need to be supplied for tonight's services."

"Pretzels," Tim countered. "You're not getting orange cheese dust all over my controllers."

"Fine." The elevator wheezed to a stop. Javi was out of the car before Tim had the second gate fully open. "See you at eight." The teen sauntered down the hallway to his family's apartment.

"Why do I have the feeling we have a supervillain in the making with that kid?" Tim slid the gates shut, and the elevator continued on its upward journey.

"Because we put too much on his shoulders," Susan replied. "Let's face it. He was Francisco, Grace, and Mitch's primary caretaker until we hired Dajon. And now, our new daycare director is down to one pre-adolescent child. And yet, who did you go to first when we bring a new child into the fold?"

"I went for the one person in this building that might understand what Harri's kid is going through."

Susan hated to admit he was right. Javi may not have powers, but he knew damn well what it felt like to lose his mom. On the other hand, Steve did have powers, and he was wavering on whether or not to suit up. He compromised by subbing for Rey and Aisha while they were in France for the next year. A test to see if he wanted and could handle such a role in his life.

The elevator groaned as it came to a halt at the fifth floor. Once again, Tim opened the gates. Susan stepped out of the car. Tim followed and closed the gates before they headed down to his and his wife's loft.

Susan sighed when she entered the spare bedroom. Harri's old queen-sized bed and the matching armoire had been shoved against the windows overlooking the parking garage. The three remaining walls minus the doors to the rest of the loft and the bath were covered with pictures, documents, and notes.

Everything pinned to the walls and the various colors of yarn linking the connections they'd traced so far had a light layer of dust. The only headway they'd made in the case was Tim's news today about someone checking out one of the kids on Mrs. Winters' list of juvenile supers.

She pulled out her phone and started taking pictures of each wall.

"That's a good idea," Tim murmured.

"Instead of Harri's office, why don't we take the boxes down to my apartment?" Susan suggested. "I can set everything back up in my spare bedroom. Especially if you guys have a houseguest longer than you expect."

Tim retrieved one of the empty banker boxes and pulled out thumbtacks. "I don't want to intrude on your personal space. Especially, if we're close to finding out what was going on with the kids that disappeared fifty years ago."

He set the pictures into the box before he pulled out his phone.

"Hola, Tim! You and Harri break your shower head again?" Men's voices and hammering nearly drowned out their building manager's voice.

Tim's face turned redder than his hair at Miguel Esperanza's teasing. "Nope. The shower's fine. What's the status on the second floor offices?"

"Only mine and one other are completed," Miguel said. "Harri instructed me to finish the other two apartments on the third floor first."

"That's fine," Tim said reassuringly. "I need the keys to the other second floor office. Harri was appointed guardian of a kid in family court today. She's been storing some legal files in our spare bedroom, and I need to move them someplace else."

"And heaven forbid she actually keeps them in the law office," Miguel grumbled.

"Hey, it's not like I'm asking you to move them," Tim shot back.

"No worries, *ese*." Miguel chuckled. "Patty has the spare keys, and Arthur has my extra hand truck."

"Thanks, Miguel. I owe you a beer." Tim tapped his phone to end the call. "I'll go get the keys and the hand truck."

"I could use one of those beers, too." Susan said.

"You deserve a six-pack every day for not running away screaming from this place." Tim grinned at her before he left.

She stared at the third wall after she finished photographing it, trying to figure out what bothered her. There was an AP file photo from the decade in question. Some fundraiser. Forever Eagle stood between Mrs. Winters and then-Captain Byron Trubble. Gil Wilcrest, the attorney who literally wrote the book on superhero law stood on Mrs. Winters' right. On Trubble's left was a much younger Rue Liberty.

Susan's phone slipped from her fingers and landed on the bedroom carpet. Oh, god, she was so dumb. They were all so dumb. The only person still alive in that picture was Rue Liberty.

Their mysterious third party couldn't possibly be anyone else.

CHAPTER 15

The smell of fear filled the rail car as they trundled toward the coast. In a lot of ways, it was more gag-inducing than the odor of Eloise's blood.

Aisha closed her eyes and tried to meditate through the stenches assaulting her olfactory nerves. It could be worse. In another hour or so, passengers were going to need to use the bathrooms.

Heavy metal poked her sternum. She opened her eyes to find their gunman staring suspiciously at her.

"Who are you trying to contact?" he demanded.

"What?" She inhaled and released the breath in an effort to calm her racing heart. All the powers in the world couldn't compensate for a person's amygdala. "I can't contact anyone. Your buddy took my phone."

"How do I know you're not a—" His last word sounded like gobbledegook.

"A what?"

"A—" Eloise repeated the word in French. "Someone who reads minds."

Aisha turned back to the gunman. "No, I'm not a telepath."

"And why should I believe you?" he sneered.

"I was trying to meditate because I really have to pee," she said. "Unless you have a contingency plan for your hostages, it's going to get smelly in here soon."

"Gah!" He stalked down the aisle to harass the other passengers.

"Thanks for putting that thought in my head." Eloise shot Aisha a weak smile.

"Sorry, but he asked." Aisha shrugged.

Eloise lowered her voice further. "What do you think will happen when we get to London?"

"I don't know," Aisha whispered. "And that's what worries me."

CHAPTER 16

Harri parked on the first floor of the Lechuza Building's garage.

"I thought we were going to your place." Diego wore a puzzled look.

She grinned. "This is my place. The law firm is on the first floor, and my loft is on the top floor." She climbed out of her car and popped the trunk.

Diego got out of the passenger side and stared at her. "Do you, like, own the whole building?"

"Only twenty-five percent of it." She handed him a couple of bags and grabbed the last two before she slammed the trunk lid shut. "One of my partners and I got an ownership interest because the owner didn't have the cash to pay his bill."

"So, you got rich representing supers?"

Harri could practically see the gears turning in Diego's head as they walked toward the entrance into the building.

She snorted. "Actually, I'm just starting to break even.

I sold everything I had left after my divorce from my first husband to start the law firm."

"How did your kids feel about you and the first Mr. Winters splitting up?"

Diego's question was a knife to her heart. She'd majorly screwed up with Eddie, and there was no way she could ever make it up to him. Even if his current wife Sarah could get over her own jealousy issues.

Harri sighed. "We didn't have any kids. That and not being honest with each other are the reasons our marriage fell apart."

"Mom and Dad fight all the time over money."

She wasn't sure what to say to that statement. She pressed her free hand against the biometric scanner. The door buzzed and clicked, and she jerked it open.

"Is that why they're both pushing you to suit up?"

"Yeah."

They entered the building. Diego looked around with detached teenage interest.

"Let me check with my office manager before we go upstairs." Harri headed for Patty's desk, and he followed her.

"Patty Ames, this is Diego Murphy. Diego, this is Patty."

The pair nodded to each other.

"Is Tim in his office?" Harri asked.

"No, he's still upstairs setting up Diego's bedroom." Patty's golden blond curls bounced as she shook her head. "He told Arthur to set up Diego so he can get in and out of the building. Tim and Susan need to talk to you about a firm matter. Arthur will escort Diego upstairs once he's finished."

Great. What had hit the fan while Harri was at the family court this afternoon?

"Thanks, Patty." Harri inclined her head in the directions of Arthur's office. "This way, Diego."

They walked past the conference room to Arthur's office. Harri knocked on the partially open door.

"Come in."

Harri pushed the door open wider and entered the room. Arthur's office looked like organized chaos, but he knew where every single piece of equipment was in his territory.

"Arthur Drallhickey, this is Diego Murphy. Diego, Arthur is the head of information technology for our law firm."

"Hey, Diego!" Unlike everyone else, Arthur wouldn't tease her about her maternal instincts.

Or lack thereof.

"I hear you'll be joining us for the next forty-five days." The slight curve of Arthur's lips would barely qualify as a smile on anyone else, but for him, it was a megawatt expression of pleasure.

"Uh, yeah, I guess."

"May I have your phone?"

Diego shot Harri a scared look.

"Don't worry. Arthur is going to check your phone for malware and install security software." She turned back to their computer guru. "Patty said you'd bring him up to the loft when you're done entering him into the system."

"I will," Arthur said solemnly.

Harri took the rest of Diego's bags and headed past the back offices for the elevator. When she reached the fifth floor, it was once again far too quiet. At this time of day, Aisha was in her own loft playing with Mitch or reading to him. The next forty-eight weeks were going to drive Harri crazy.

She entered her own loft, but no one was in the living area. "Tim! Susan!"

"Back here!"

Harri dropped the shopping bags and her purse on her couch and stalked back to the spare bedroom. And stopped dead in the doorway. The room no longer looked like an obsessed detective's den.

Or like a serial killer's.

The furniture had been rearranged to make it actually look like a boy's bedroom. A navy blue comforter she didn't recognize covered the bed. A black metal stand from the Owl's Nest held a TV and gaming console, all of which were hooked up. One of hers and Tim's gaming chairs sat in front of the console. The walls were bare, but Diego could put up posters of whatever hot fad held him in its grip. Everything had been dusted and the carpet vacuumed.

"Wow!" Harri shook her head. "I can't believe you two got all this done in a couple of hours."

"Well, Steve and Nick handled the furniture rearranging

once we moved the boxes down to the spare office on the second floor," Susan said.

"And she took photos of the placement of pictures and notes, so we can set everything up the way you had it," Tim added.

Thank heavens, Tim used the interns and didn't try to move the furniture by himself. Not that Harri could ever say that in front of her husband. She'd learned her lesson about trying to protect him long ago.

"That is a better idea than my home office." She relaxed and leaned against the door frame "Is that what you guys wanted to tell me in private?"

"No." Susan glanced at Tim.

"The floor's yours," he said.

A burr of anxiety wormed its way up Harri's spine. Please don't say you're quitting. Please don't say you're quitting.

Susan crossed her arms. "Yesterday morning, Eddie and an NSB agent took me and Sparx out to a body dump in the desert. The person was murdered execution style and buried in a shallow grave."

"Two federal agencies working together?" Tim frowned.

"They're waiting on the DNA results, but both Consuelo and Nesmith think it was Trubble." Susan exhaled.

Harri wasn't sure what bothered her more—that Trubble may have come to such an ignominious end, that the heads of the FBI and NSB office dragged Susan and a client out in the middle of the desert, or that her so-called partner was just now telling her about the incident.

"Harri, they swore me and Sparx to silence because they were concerned you might—"

"Might what?" she growled.

"Do something to impede their investigation," Susan said.

"How could you do something so stupid!" Harri exploded. "Sparx may generate gigawatts of power, but none of it goes to her brain. I expect better from you!"

"I know. That is why I told you. I know you have trust issues—"

"This goes beyond my trust issues, Susan," Harri snapped. "Beyond the fiduciary duty legal partners have to each other. Information is life and death with us, our staff, and our clients. You should have been suspicious of both the NSB and the FBI—"

"Dammit, I was, Harri." Susan threw her hands in the air. "Even more so when I saw they'd already dragged Sparx into the mix. Why do you think I went with Eddie out to the desert?"

"Don't drag my ex into this." Harri shook her head.

"I'm not—" Susan took a deep breath. "Do you think anyone would have told us they found Trubble's corpse if Sparx and I hadn't accompanied them? What do you think Nesmith would have done if Aisha was still in the country? He's already threatened to out Rey to get you two to go along with whatever he wants. As for Consuelo, she's still cleaning up the mess at the local FBI office."

"You think that makes her innocent?"

"No, not one bit. Not when she already figured out Aisha is the Ghost Owl. But I don't think either agent is out to get us."

"What do you mean?" Harri asked.

"This was their way of testing to make sure neither of my legal partners were the ones who executed Trubble and left him in a shallow grave."

Harri swallowed hard. "Y-you actually think I would—"

Susan folded her arms across her chest. "If it meant saving someone you loved, then yes. I think you're more than capable of killing."

Harri couldn't stop her shaking. Because Susan was right. And god help her, she knew if it came to Tim or Aisha or Jeremy or anyone she considered family, she would do anything to protect them.

"You don't trust me," Harri stated flatly.

Susan shook her head. "It's not that simple. There's something else you should know. I have reason to believe Rue Liberty is our mysterious third party who is looking for the missing super kids. Nesmith is fairly certain your grandmother was funding Forever Eagle's Underground Railroad for supers." She turned to Tim. "The computer search for the dead kid came up on his radar, too."

"You still should have told me all of this yesterday."

Harri shook. And she thought she wanted to hit someone earlier this afternoon.

"Harri—"

"I need you to leave my loft before I do something we all regret."

Susan clamped her mouth shut and strode out of the bedroom. Only when Harri heard the loft door roll shut did she let loose her tears of fury. She hated the fact she cried when she was pissed as hell.

Tim crossed to her and pulled her into his arms. Thankfully, he said nothing because she wasn't sure what she'd do to him if he did.

CHAPTER 17

<hr>

Susan went to her own apartment and changed clothes. She didn't let herself think. If she did, she'd do something stupid.

Like quit Winters and Franklin, just like she had quit Dewey and Cheatham when they screwed her out of her bonus.

It was just a fight, but even her inner voice didn't sound too convinced.

Had Harri even listened to what Susan said about Rue Liberty? Or was she too outraged Susan had waited nearly thirty-six hours before she confessed to her little field trip with the feds?

Did any of it really matter?

If she left the law firm, she could help Dad take care of Mom. Her family wouldn't be targeted anymore if she was no longer affiliated with Winters and Franklin.

But it would also mean giving up her retirement dream of a little boutique in the new Canyon Block shopping plaza.

Rey wouldn't want to deal with someone who betrayed his wife and his wife's best friend.

That's what it came down to, wasn't it? Harri and Aisha had been BFFs since they were in elementary school. Susan was the third wheel. Someone they only depended on to keep clients happy and do the grunt work.

She really needed an objective opinion. She pulled her phone out of her jeans pocket and dialed Dad's number before she flopped on her couch.

"Hey, baby doll. Long time, no hear."

"Hey, Dad." The words choked her.

"What's wrong?" Alarm filled his voice. "Are you okay? Did a supervillain break into the office?"

"No, it's nothing like that." She sniffed. "I'm trying to pull up my big girl panties, but I need some advice."

"Okay, shoot."

Susan told him about the incident with the feds yesterday and her argument with Harri a little while ago.

"Trubble's the black ops jerk you think was behind the break-in at the cabin, right? And he's tried to kill both Harri and Aisha?"

"Yeah." It scared her to think of what could have happened to her parents and her sister's family if Trubble had the guys who broke-in do more than vandalize her parents' vacation cabin in the mountains a year ago last Christmas.

Dad's breath came out in a whoosh. "Well, I can kind of understand why Harri's a little miffed you waited to tell her."

"I'm not even certain it was Trubble they found. We won't know until the FBI finishes the DNA testing."

"Baby doll, I'm in a similar situation," he murmured. "I can't lie to your mom to protect her. That pisses her off because she knows something's wrong even though she can't remember what it is from one moment to the next."

"Speaking of mom, where is she?"

"Napping. I'm out on the deck reading." He chuckled. "Don't worry. I have motion sensors that beep when she gets out of bed."

"What if I move in with you and help take care of Mom?"

"No."

"But Dad—"

"You're not moving in with us out of guilt because you lied by omission to Harri," he said sternly. "Besides, we've already selected an assisted living community."

"Now, who's lying by omission?" Susan teased.

"We signed the paperwork this morning, which is why your mom was tuckered out." He sighed. "You and your sister don't need to be wasting your lives taking care of us. We had a nice long chat with the Tranhs. We're moving in next door to them."

"And what exactly did you and Qiang's parents discuss?"

Dad chuckled again. "Mainly, they're glad their daughter has found love again after the tragic loss of her husband. And they talked about their own guilt at not being able to help more with their grandson."

"And?" Susan prompted.

"It's nice to have someone to talk to about your spouse's health issues without driving your family crazy."

"And?" Susan asked again.

"We don't want to do the same thing to you they did to Qiang."

"From her perspective, she did everything for them out of love," Susan murmured.

"I know you and Tracy would do the same for us, but it's still not fair to put all the burden on you girls. You have your own lives. You need to live them. Even if it means kissing Harri's ass for the rest of the week and promising never to withhold information from her ever again."

Susan laughed. "All right, Dad. I hear you."

After she ended the call, she stared at the ceiling. Dad may be right, but would Harri listen to, much less accept, her apology?

CHAPTER 18

Outside the rail car, lights flickered by in time to the rhythm of the steel wheels beneath them. They were officially in the Chunnel, the tunnel beneath the English Channel connecting mainland Europe with the British Isles.

Aisha checked Eloise's wrist again. She didn't need to touch it to know the blood circulation in the limb had stopped. Not from the way her fingers were turning blue. At least, the poor woman could sleep.

Aisha's mind kept running through the worst possible scenarios. Was the gunmen and his accomplices planning on simply killing all the passengers to make a political statement? Was there a bomb on board? Was it C4 or a dirty nuke? Were they planning on destroying the Chunnel? Or worse, did they have some kind of poison or biological agent and they planned to deploy it in London?

Did she use her powers to stop whatever was about to happen? What if her only option was escaping?

Maybe she should borrow the aluminum briefcase from

the man across the aisle from her and Eloise. It would make more of a dent in the gunman's skull than her soft-sided case. She just needed the right opportunity.

As if in answer to her prayers, the train slowed. The lights in both the Chunnel and their car cut out, and they were plunged into darkness.

"Nobody move," the gunman yelled.

But Aisha was already moving. She snatched the metal briefcase from the man across the aisle. The red emergency lights flickered on. She swung the metal case at the gunman's head. He dropped like the proverbial sack of potatoes. She kicked his rifle to the side. Her phone's power cord would have to do for restraining the jerk.

Aisha took one step toward her seat when armed people poured into the car from the back and the exterior door.

"Police! Everyone on the floor with your hands up!"

Relief washed through her at someone speaking English, even if it was a U.K. accent.

"Bloody hell!" One of the officers turned over the gunman. "He's out cold."

Another officer looked at the aluminum case, then at a kneeling Aisha with her hands in the air.

"Yes, I hit him. He shot my seatmate Eloise." She inclined her head toward the injured woman before she let the officers cuff her and escort her from the train.

At least, she hadn't used her powers.

CHAPTER 19

Harri couldn't say she was calm when Arthur escorted Diego to her loft a half hour later. But she could be pleasant to the teen. She started a load of laundry with Diego's new underwear before she suggested they walk down to Marta's for dinner.

The restaurant was packed when Harri, Tim, and Diego entered, but the back booth was empty. Marta kept it free because it was the one place where a patron could keep an eye on all the doors and windows at the same time. Convenient for the staff and clients of Winters and Franklin who all affectionately nicknamed the table Tim's Nest.

"Is Kordell working tonight?" Harri asked as Marta set menus and napkin-wrapped silverware in front of her.

"Yes, but can you wait until the crowd dies down before you steal another one of my cooks?" Marta rolled her eyes.

"Of course." Harri splayed her over her upper chest. "You know I'd never interfere with my own meal."

Marta laughed and headed back to the front. Her youngest daughter took their orders and brought their drinks to the table. It wasn't hard to miss Diego checking out Anna.

"Dude," Tim whispered. "She's in college and a little too old for you."

The kid grinned. "Maybe she likes them young and trainable."

Harri slouched in her seat. Maybe introducing Javi to Diego was a really bad idea.

"Are you in any activities at school?" Tim asked.

"They're all lame." That seemed to be his excuse for anything he didn't want to do. "Where's the bathroom in this joint?"

Tim and Harri pointed to their right. Diego slid out of the booth and trudged down the corridor leading to the public restrooms.

"I take his parents are real pieces of work," Tim murmured.

"That's putting it mildly." Harri shook her head. "The teen years are hard enough, but when your parents just don't give a shit except for what you can do for them . . ."

"Ouch." Tim played with his silverware before he said, "Don't you think you were a little hard on Susan?"

"She's already on my shit list, Canyon. Don't make me add you, too," Harri warned.

"Is Nesmith on your shit list?" Tim's right eyebrow rose. "Or did he inform you about his little meeting with Susan and Qiang when he saw you at court?"

Harri turned away and toyed with the condensation on her glass of ice tea. She hated when her husband was right. "It's not the same. Nesmith isn't my partner."

"But you're acting exactly how he feared, which is why he didn't want to tell you about the body they found."

Harri glared at him. "You knew about it?" Of course, he did. Tim and Arthur had infiltrated the NSB computer system ages ago in their attempts to find Rey after he'd been kidnapped.

Tim shrugged. "Yes, Arthur and I did. We're waiting to see if the FBI could confirm the corpse's identity before we said anything to you. And we did it for the same reasons."

"I hate you," she muttered.

"I love you, too," he replied.

They remained silent until Anna brought out their plates.

"What the heck is Diego doing in the bathroom?"

Tim set his silverware and napkin back on the table. "I'll go check."

But before he could rise, Kordell escorted Diego to their booth by the kid's ear.

"You lose something, Harri?" Kordell scowled beneath the hairnet that kept his short braids out of his face while he manned the grill. He guided Diego into the booth and then sat beside the teen so he couldn't escape. "I hate it when you make me sit on this side, Canyon."

Tim merely grinned at Kordell's complaint.

"What did he do?" Harri asked.

"He was back by the dumpster, setting cockroaches on fire." Thankfully, Kordell Lyons, AKA Shadowstar, was savvy enough not to mention how Diego was setting things on fire.

"Did anyone see him?"

"Nah, but he learned real quick that his tricks don't work on me." Kordell grinned at the teen.

"Well, I wanted him to meet you, but not like this." Harri made the official introductions.

Kordell held out his palm. Diego eyed it like the super had offered a scorpion.

"It's good manners to shake someone's hand." Kordell lowered his voice. "Especially if you just tried to incinerate him, and he didn't retaliate."

Diego tentatively grasped Kordell's hand and shook it. A brilliant grin flashed across the man's dark face. He looked at Harri.

"I take it he's why you wanted to talk to me?"

"Yep. I wanted him to meet you and Steve so he realizes he has different options in life," she said. "Do you have some time this week?"

"How about I stop by for a little bit tonight after the dinner rush?"

Tim laughed. "Emilio still asking for extra hours?"

Kordell held up his palms. "Hey, if the kid wants to clean the grill every night, it's no skin off my back. I'll see you about nine." He rose and sauntered back to the kitchen.

"Why is he a cook at a tiny restaurant?" Diego asked.

"That's his story to tell." Harri shrugged. "Like I said, I know a lot of different types of people. But when we get home, we need to talk about limits and the proper time and place to display your tricks."

"Yes, ma'am." For all his protestations that he wasn't hungry, the teen was the first one to clean his plate and devour Marta's dessert specialty, mocha cinnamon mousse.

CHAPTER 20

Aisha answered the London police's questions repeatedly. They didn't seem satisfied with her responses. Finally, a higher ranking officer came in and said she'd been released.

A woman with a stern expression waited for her in the lobby. She was a couple of inches shorter than Aisha, with dark hair pulled back in a tight bun, a no-nonsense gray business suit, and black sensible pumps. She was also holding Aisha's two bags. She stepped forward and held out her hand.

"Ms. Franklin, I'm Tessa McKinney from Amblehurst, Mintegue, and Trott. Come with me please."

"Ms. McKinney." Aisha shook the woman's hand. "How did you know I was here?"

The other woman shrugged. "The partners' have their ways. But if it's all right, it's better we discuss things in the car."

"How about I carry my bags?" Aisha waved at the straps

over Tessa's shoulder. "You didn't happen to get my phone back from the police, did you?"

"Yes, I did." Tessa pulled the device from her purse and handed it to Aisha as well as her bags.

She followed the other woman out to the parking lot. Tessa drove a nondescript sedan. Aisha quelled a shiver. The vehicle reminded her too much of the cars the NSB used.

"Did you get any information from the police about what was going on in the train?"

Tessa's lips quirked up as she pulled into traffic. "Only that you rightly bashed one of the terrorists in the noggin."

Aisha sighed. "In all fairness, he had already shot one of the other passengers."

"Do you always take on armed men?" Tessa asked.

"Only when they plan to shoot me."

"I shall endeavor not to point a gun at you." Tessa glanced at Aisha. "What would you have done if it had been a super?"

"I don't know," Aisha murmured. The same question had been running through her mind for the last several hours. She looked at Tessa. "Are you an attorney at the firm?"

"No, ma'am, I'm a member of the security team."

"It's not 'ma'am', just Aisha."

"All right, just Aisha. I'm Tessa."

"Can you drop me off at my hotel? I have reservations at—"

"No, my orders were to take you straight to the firm's main office. Mr. Amblehurst wishes to speak with you first."

"This late?"

Tessa shrugged. "My orders were directly from him."

Ten minutes later, Tessa pulled into a parking garage. Unsure of what was going on, Aisha grabbed her bags and followed Tessa. She led the way into the building, which had security similar to their own building back home. Tessa ushered Aisha into a conference room.

All five people in the room were dressed in proper business attire despite the late, or rather, early morning hours. The balding middle-aged man at the end of the table stood and smiled at her.

"Welcome to Amblehurst, Mintegue, and Trott, Ms. Franklin. I'm Benedict Amblehurst. Please have a seat."

Aisha remained standing. Something stunk here. "I'm a little confused, Mr. Amblehurst. I thought we were supposed to meet at ten a.m. London time."

"After your performance under pressure, we wanted to move ahead with our meeting."

"My performance under pressure?"

"We have some concerns about partnering with an American firm when one of the partners shows violent tendencies."

"You think I have violent tendencies?" Did they know about her alter ego?

"Actually, we are concerned about your partner Harriet

Winters," Amblehurst said. "Given that she used a gun on an intruder at her own wedding—"

"When that intruder threatened to shoot my husband," Aisha bit out.

"Nevertheless, we are relieved to see you have a level head—"

"Excuse me. How exactly should I have reacted on the train?" She crossed her arms.

"Frankly, we didn't expect you to take matters into your own hands—"

"What should I have done?"

"Waited for appropriate assistance." Amblehurst gestured emphatically. "Saving people is our clients' purpose in life."

Aisha stared at him as everything clicked into place. "Those weren't terrorists? You were testing me?"

"Lightstreak is looking only at the money. He doesn't understand his kind need to be controlled and nurtured for the good of mankind."

Amblehurst's statement sounded too much like Trubble's BS.

"What's the problem with licensing his image for the good of mankind?"

The British attorney didn't seem to get her sarcasm. "You are going to steal our clients Ms. Franklin, the way you swooped in on your former employer's."

The conference room door opened, and a man and a

woman walked in. Aisha's mouth fell open as she recognized the woman who called herself Eloise. There wasn't a damn thing wrong with her.

"You're wicked with a briefcase." The man grinned at her. "Five stitches in my scalp, love."

Her blood froze. He was the gunman. It was a setup. The whole damn thing was a setup. It didn't matter why.

She stepped closer to him. "Come near me, my family, or my clients again, and I'll do more than hit you with a briefcase, asshole."

Aisha turned to the head partner. "How's that for violent tendencies, Mr. Amblehurst?" Somehow, she resisted the urge to turn the conference room door to dust as she marched out.

CHAPTER 21

When Susan returned from her fast food run, she stood and stared at her living room. She didn't blame Harri one bit for being pissed at her or questioning her loyalties. Maybe she needed to pack her personal things and turn in her resignation despite what Dad had said. This job was drowning her.

There was a knock on her door. She considered ignoring it, but if Harri wanted to fire her, maybe it was better to get it over with now. She had no illusions that Aisha would side with her. Not against Aisha's best friend.

Instead of Harri, Qiang, Steve, and the rest of the interns burst into Susan's apartment.

"You can't leave the firm!" Qiang grabbed Susan's arm and dragged her to her couch.

Maybe she should be thankful Qiang didn't accidentally electrocute her in the superhero's agitated state.

"What are you all doing here?" Susan looked at each person.

Steve crossed his arms. "We're trying to keep Winters and Franklin from falling apart. Which is exactly what the bad guys want to happen."

"Look, you guys, I appreciate the concern, but this has nothing to do with the bad guys—"

"I got a text from Rey. The meeting with Amblehurst, Mintegue, and Trott was a set up. First, they hired some thugs to hijack Aisha's train and scare her. Then, they accused her of trying to poach their clients."

The only other time Susan had seen Steve that furious was when the subject of Professor Paranoia came up.

"Did she use her powers in front of the hired thugs?"

"No, but she's mad as hell, and Rey's got his hands full calming her down."

"If you leave, there's no way Harri can run this place with just her and Travis," Bethany said. "We all know Aisha will do her best, but the eight-hour difference between Paris and Canyon Pointe means she can't jump on things in real time."

"What were really trying to say is please don't leave us alone with Harri," Nick begged. "This place does good work. And y'all don't try to rip off your clients."

"We like that you guys are ethical," Mariah added. "Your clients like that you're ethical. The only time there's a problem is when you three bicker like sisters."

"Sisters?" A lump grew in Susan's throat.

"Yeah," Qiang grinned. "Sisters. Now, are you going to

suck it up and stay? Or do I have to tattle to your mom and dad?"

"You know about them moving to the same facility as your parents?"

Qiang nodded. "Mom and Dad are pretty excited to have another couple there that they know."

"All right." Susan held up her hands in surrender. "You guys win. I'll stay."

And maybe, just maybe, she and Harri could work out their issues.

Chapter 22

The next morning, Aisha sat on the couch totally unsure of what to do with her fury. She hadn't wanted to fire Delphine. Hell, the girl cried and begged, but Aisha had no way of telling whether or not they were crocodile tears. As much of a pain Mother Defiant was as a client, Aisha could definitely use the super's truth-telling abilities right now.

Rey walked into the living room. "Mitch is down for his nap." When she didn't answer, he sat next to her, wrapped his arms around her, and pulled her close. "Talk to me, baby."

But she couldn't relax into his arms. "I could have blown both of our identities on that train."

"But you didn't, and no one was really hurt," he murmured against her hair. "You did the right thing by keeping your head down."

"Amblehurst didn't have to set me up like that."

"No, they shouldn't have." He leaned his forehead against her hair. "I'm thankful you found out what shits they are before you and your partners signed anything with them."

"I hate them for making me question Delphine's integrity."

"So do I, baby. I didn't want to fire her, but I understand why you had to do it."

Aisha looked up at him. Unshed tears glimmered in her eyes. "I hate even more that Harri was right. I can't work full-time and watch Mitch. Do I call Molly and suck up to her?"

"We can try, but don't be surprised if she tells us to do anatomically impossible things with ourselves."

His comment forced a giggle to slip from Aisha. She swiped at the tears that escaped down her cheeks.

"So what should we do?"

"Take a day or two, and just relax." He stroked her dreds. "You'll think of something. You always do."

"I still need to tell Harri and Susan what happened." God, she dreaded that conversation. She'd never questioned her legal instincts or skills until now.

"I know you do, but it's the middle of the night in Canyon Pointe. Let them get a good night's sleep before you dump your very bad day on them."

"All right." She snuggled into her husband's embrace. "Besides, I'll need Susan to talk me and Harri down from some kind of awful revenge against Amblehurst, Mintegue, and Trott."

CHAPTER 23

The following evening, the scent of pepperoni and oregano filled Harri's loft. Kordell had picked up pizzas on his way over, his first lesson on how to bond with teenage boys. And despite Diego's protestations that Foxstar was a lame game, a tournament had started between slices.

"Take that!" Harri tapped the button for her ship's blasters as fast as she could on her controller.

"You two don't have a chance," Kordell retorted. His fighter zipped out of her firing range.

"Get her, Kordell!" Diego yelled as he blew up the fuel depot.

"You little rat!" Javi dramatically flopped on the floor as the TV screen displayed his ship crashing and exploding on the planet's surface after his ship was caught in Diego's pyromaniacal act.

Harri's phone rang as she blasted asteroids and planetary defense weapons with equal glee in a desperate effort to redeem her teammate's honor. "Honey, would you get that?"

Behind her, Tim said, "Hey, Serena! What's up?" There was a pause before his tone changed. "Are you shitting me? All right. We're on our way."

The conversation was just enough of a distraction. Diego's ship dropped out of hyperspace right in front of Harri's vessel. She fumbled with the shield control as he fired. Her ship exploded in a dazzling array of graphic fireballs.

Kordell and Diego cheered and high-fived each other.

Harri climbed to her feet. "What's wrong at Serena's?"

Even Kordell sobered and stood. "You need backup, man?"

"No." Tim grabbed his and Harri's jackets hanging on the pegs by the loft door. "But could you stay here until we get back? She's got a rat problem."

"We don't need a babysitter." Diego jutted his chin out in raw defiance.

"Not a babysitter," Harri said as she slipped on her jacket. "Someone to guard my food. I've seen the way you and Javi eat."

Kordell picked up on Tim's hint. "Let's keep playing, Diego. Javi needs the practice."

"Hey!" Javi protested as Tim rolled back the loft door and gestured for Harri to exit.

She waited until she and her husband were on the elevator and headed down to the first floor before she said, "Is Serena okay?"

"Yeah, she knocked out Monica with her powers." Tim

typed on his phone. No doubt sending a text to Arthur and Steve to warn them what was up.

"Your ex showed up on Serena's doorstep?" Harri stared at him in disbelief.

Tim groaned. "I really wish you would stop calling her that. It didn't even qualify as an affair. At least, she didn't show up in our loft this time."

Harri hugged herself. "We need to call the NSB."

"Monica's not stupid enough to come anywhere near you after she double-crossed Carol Inunza and kidnapped Trubble unless she's really desperate." Tim sighed. "Serena said Monica was hurt pretty bad."

"So whoever she was working for decided she was expendable, too." The elevator ground to a stop, and Harri yanked open the gates. "We'd better hope they think she's dead. Otherwise—"

"We need to get Serena and Celia someplace safe," Tim said.

"What about Monica?"

Tim pursed his lips and said nothing.

Five minutes later, Harri and Tim were climbing the stairs to Serena's third floor walk-up. The physician assistant's front door opened before either of them could knock.

"In here." Serena inclined her head. Her dark skin, silver hair, and pajamas were flecked with blood spots.

Monica Reinhold, AKA Miss Purrception, sprawled across Serena's faux Persian rug in the middle of the living room. More blood coated the green, black, and cream pattern, and Harri was pretty sure the shiny spots on Monica's black unitard was blood, too.

Serena had placed a pillow beneath the supervillain's head.

"Is she still alive?" Harri asked.

"Barely." The physician's assistant collapsed on her couch. "She had three gunshot wounds. One so close to the heart, I had a rough time removing it so I could heal her."

"You should have let her die."

Harri looked at her husband. That wasn't like Tim. "You don't mean that."

"He's right, Harri," Monica said. "It would have been a lot easier for all of us."

Harri looked at the supervillain lying on the floor. "That's not like you either. But if you want our help you'd better start spilling the truth."

Tears leaked from the corners of Monica's eyes. "I should have known once she decided to kill Trubble, I would be next on her list. No loose ends."

"Who?" Harri demanded.

"My mother," Monica whispered. "Your precious Rue Liberty."

Now that the truth is out about who Grandma Harri was hiding the child supers from, how do the partners and staff at Winters and Franklin bring down one of the most famous and celebrated superheroes alive?

Turn the page to read an excerpt from the next volume:

Queer Eye for the Super Guy!

QUEER EYE FOR THE SUPER GUY

Jeremy Harkness examined the business plan his husband Leonardo had set on the counter while he chopped mushrooms for their breakfast omelets. The idea was sound, but . . .

He set aside the knife and looked up at Leonardo who perched on a stool on the opposite side of their kitchen island. "But why, darling?"

"Why, what?" Leonardo frowned.

"I don't understand why you'd want to design for the hoi polloi, baby doll," Jeremy answered.

"The general public is not the hoi polloi, and no offense—" Leonardo hesitated a moment before he blurted, "I want a little something to call my own. I hate feeling like I'm riding on your dress train."

"You're not—" Jeremy started to protest.

"If we don't promote Elaine, she's going to leave to start her own salon." Leonardo pantomimed trading one thing for another. "Besides Rey already set aside space for us in the new Canyon Block shopping complex."

Rey Garcia, aka the superhero Black Falcon, was generous to a fault. He'd finally managed to close on the city block that had housed Canyon Industries, Canyon Pointe's largest employer until the company collapsed nearly three decades ago. Rey was making sure the homeless folks he knew had jobs and places to live since he had been one of them not so long ago.

Not to mention Rey made Jeremy's foster sister Aisha so damn happy. It was hard to hate the man for being good-looking and a total sweetheart, too.

Jeremy nodded. "All right. We can withdraw the money from one of our money market funds—"

"No." Leonardo held up his right palm. "I've already set aside the capital I will need."

"Leonardo Chen Harkness!" Jeremy laid his palm on his chest. "You have secret money I don't know about?"

"Quit being a drama queen." Leonardo scowled. "I've been squirreling away money in my fun account for years."

Jeremy bit his lower lip. He'd been the one to insist they have separate accounts for their own personal use so neither of them had to justify such spending to the other spouse. His bio parents had some rather nasty fights over Dad's race track betting and Mom's shoe shopping before they tossed Jeremy out of the house. He sighed. The 'rents probably still had those same fights.

"Don't give me the sigh of disbelief," Leonardo said crossly.

Jeremy leaned his elbows on the counter and took Leonardo's hands in his. "It was the sigh of self-disgust that I was on the verge of acting like my bio 'rents. And for that, I sincerely apologize, my love."

Leonardo flashed a sweet smile. "All's forgiven." He leaned closer and pecked Jeremy on the lips.

"Can I see some of your designs?" Jeremy asked when they parted.

"Not yet," Leonardo said.

A little twinge of anxiety raced along Jeremy's nerves. He knew it was a stupid reaction to what Ryan had done to him twenty years ago. And it definitely wasn't fair to compare that asshole to Leonardo.

"I'm actually working with Susan Kennedy," Leonardo continued. "She's been designing jewelry on the side."

"She is?" Jeremy blinked, but he didn't know why he was surprised. His foster sisters' law partner was a fountain of odd talents. "Wait a minute! Was she where you came up with the idea for the earring comms for the supers?"

Leonardo nodded. "I said one set she showed me was big enough to hide Timmy's equipment, and we got to talking."

Jeremy was a big enough queen to admit his feelings were hurt, but he also wanted his husband to be happy. "Just make sure you have someone else look over any partnership papers before you sign anything."

Leonardo's eyes widened. "Do you really think Susan would screw me over?"

Jeremy chuckled. "Only if she really wants Harri and Aisha to pound the crap out of her. But this is your baby, and I'll stay out of your way, muffin."

His phone chose that moment to dance along the surface of the island's granite countertop to the tune of Helen Reddy's "I Am Woman." Even odder was the caller ID showed Melanie's personal number, not their alter ego, Ultramegaperson.

He tapped the answer icon. "What's up, doll?"

"I have a personal question for you and a request," the throaty voice of the world's most powerful super said. "Remember that producer Dale I've been dating?"

"You've mentioned him." Jeremy grabbed his phone and stepped back to lean against the sink counter. Leonardo pulled the cutting board towards himself and started mincing the garlic.

"He wants to know if my designer would like to be involved in a nationally televised reality show where eight designers for superheroes would compete to dress twelve brand-new supers."

"Mel, you know I like my privacy when it comes to designing supersuits," Jeremy said.

"Which is the reason I'm calling you instead of my boyfriend Dale calling you." Mel gave an exaggerated sigh. "You know I'd be the last person on the planet to out your secret designing skills, but since you design for a large number of other heroes, he really wants you to participate in his show."

"What's the catch?" Jeremy said.

"One of the twelve people the contestants will be designing for is a supervillain."

Preorder *Queer Eye for the Super Guy* at your favorite retailer!

Want a sneak peek at the special Crossover novel *Invasion!*? Turn the page!

INVASION!

Author's Note: *Invasion!* takes place after the events in *Queer Eye for the Super Guy*.

Veteran's Memorial Park, Canyon Pointe, State of Mojave, the week before Christmas

Aisha Franklin, the superhero known publicly as the Ghost Owl, winced as the talons of the creature she fought tore through her uniform, and worse into the skin of her thigh. Her hero togs were made out of material stronger and suppler than Kevlar. Not to mention, her skin was damn near invulnerable.

She punched at what appeared to be the creature's head. Her fist went through the head as if it had phased its molecules like fellow superhero Shadowstar. But when she tried to pull back, her arm was stuck inside the creature.

Fine. Let's see how it handled supersonic speed. She flew straight up, dragging the creature with her. Her predecessor as the Ghost Owl had literally designed a variation of her suit for NASA. The repair systems had already ejected sealant along the rips, so she wouldn't have any issues as the atmosphere thinned. For all her powers, she still needed to breathe. The heads up display inside her helmet ticked off the altitude.

At ten miles above the earth's surface, the creature phased, and her arm slipped free of its head. The thing may be able to phase, but gravity was still queen. It plummeted. Aisha dove after it.

It fell towards a thunderstorm developing east of the city. While it probably wouldn't hit anybody in the state park on the other side of Lake Del Oro from the city, she couldn't take the chance. She poured on speed. Static built along her suit in the unstable atmosphere.

Lightning erupted between her and the clouds below. Her suit was insulated from the surge in electricity. But the creature was caught in the bolt of lightning.

Aisha grinned to herself as the thing disintegrated in the one-point-twenty-one gigawatts of Mother Nature's power. One down. She needed to get back to Canyon Pointe. She headed west and flew as fast as she could. No doubt complaints would be filed for the sonic booms from her wake.

In Veterans' Memorial Park, the CPPD were trying to clear the area of civilians who were still on their feet. EMTs attempted to treat and evacuate the people who had been mauled by these things. It was up to Aisha to keep these creatures occupied and away from the population of the city until backup came.

Relief spread through her when Sparx's voice crackled through the speakers in Aisha's helmet. "What the hell are these things?"

"You got me," Aisha replied. "Don't let them get near you. I just got raked by their claws. But the one I dealt with didn't like lightning much." She grabbed a couple of kids hiding behind a tree and delivered them to waiting officers without a word.

"Roger that." Sparx's crisp answer was almost drowned out by Nix's sonic shriek.

"Think Doctor Triassic has been experimenting?" Aisha asked.

"Don't know, but whatever they are, they smell worse than the snake exhibit at the zoo," Sparx said.

Aisha's Ghost Owl suit was designed by her predecessor to filter out toxins when she was in normal earth atmosphere, so she didn't get a hint of whatever Sparx picked up.

"Guys, they don't like water either," Nix said. "I knocked one into the fountain, and I think it died."

Aisha's visor darkened as Sparx cut loose on a third creature now that the park was clear of civilians.

"How many are left?" Sparx asked.

Aisha rose a few feet above the grass and spun to scan the area. "I see two more by the pin oak grove." She flew in that direction.

And was horrified to see a civilian lying on the ground between the two creatures.

"Sparx!"

"Right behind you. You kick them away from the guy, and I'll blast them."

Aisha was fast enough the creatures didn't have a chance to phase. She literally kicked the one on the right straight up into the air, tearing out a great deal of green foliage as it arrowed upward. Lightning flashed behind her. She reached for the other one as it sliced its talons across the throat of the unconscious young man laying beneath the tree. There was a weird chittering cough sound from the creature as she grabbed what appeared to be its throat.

Her suit's radiation alarms blared for a second before all the suit systems died. The only thing Aisha knew for sure was that she and the creature were falling, tumbling through empty space with no idea of which way was up.

Acknowledgements

As always, I owe so much to my cover artist Elaina Lee and my formatter J.W. Manus. Without these awesome ladies, I would be flipping burgers. Or worse, practicing law.

Much love to Darling Husband for keeping me fed while I was on several deadlines this spring and to Princess Bella for reminding me treats and belly rubs are necessary for a good life.

And to my readers, thank you for following the adventures of the lawyers and clients of Winters & Franklin through ten books!

About the Author

Suzan Harden transitioned from writing information technology manuals for companies and legal articles for a law enforcement magazine to her first love, fantasy and science fiction in all their forms. She's the author of the Bloodlines, the 888-555-HERO, and the Justice series.

www.ingramcontent.com/pod-product-compliance
Lightning Source LLC
Chambersburg PA
CBHW060554100726
47907CB00005B/1357